TOURMALINE

AND THE ISLAND OF ELSEWHERE

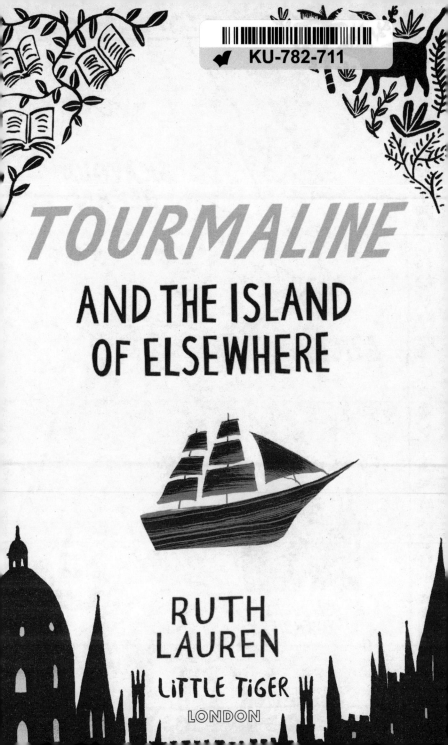

RUTH LAUREN

LITTLE TIGER

LONDON

TOURMALINE
AND THE ISLAND OF ELSEWHERE

This book is for Leo and so is the cat.
RL

LITTLE TIGER

An imprint of Little Tiger Press Limited

1 Coda Studios, 189 Munster Road, London SW6 6AW

Imported into the EEA by Penguin Random House Ireland,
Morrison Chambers, 32 Nassau Street, Dublin D02 YH68

www.littletiger.co.uk

First published in Great Britain in 2023

Text copyright © Ruth Lauren, 2023
Illustrations copyright © Sharon King-Chai, 2023

ISBN: 978-1-78895-591-1

The Forest Stewardship Council® (FSC®) is a global, not-for-profit organization dedicated to the
promotion of responsible forest management worldwide. FSC defines standards based on agreed principles
for responsible forest stewardship that are supported by environmental, social, and economic stakeholders.
To learn more, visit www.fsc.org

2 4 6 8 10 9 7 5 3 1

Chapter One

It was Professor Aladeus's own fault that Tourmaline was on her way to spy on him. If he hadn't given her that strange look on his way past the music room before hurrying on into the depths of the university, she wouldn't be crawling through a particularly narrow part of the space-between to reach his study.

She had discovered the space-between by accident after almost getting caught in one of the (strictly out-of-bounds) display rooms of the university museum. She'd had to hide in a mercifully empty sarcophagus, which she'd quickly found wasn't a sarcophagus at all – at least, it wasn't *only* a sarcophagus. She'd rolled right out of it into the space-between, and learned that hidden inside Pellavere University's walls was a possibly magical echo of its many dusty halls and corridors. The space-between had since proved to be very useful indeed.

However, the wonder of its existence wasn't in the forefront of her mind as she reached her destination. She left via the exit in the master's study and crouched uncomfortably inside the musty magician's disappearing box. It was getting to be quite a squeeze since she'd turned twelve but she wasn't about to let a little thing like size get in her way.

Professor Aladeus was already there, pacing, and he wasn't alone.

"There's been no contact at all?" The other person was Professor Sharma, the Geography professor, who was much younger and much taller and much more nervous than Professor Aladeus.

"Nothing for an entire week," said Professor Aladeus. "Simply vanished without a trace." His voice was high and clear so Tourmaline's sharp ears had no trouble hearing him from her hiding place.

Tourmaline had arrived partway through the conversation, so she didn't know who or what had vanished, which was an inconvenience, but one she decided not to hold against either professor since she hadn't exactly been invited to take part in the discussion.

"And are we … attempting a rescue mission?" Professor Sharma sounded nervous.

There was a pause and then a terse answer. "Where would you suggest we send them?"

Professor Aladeus recommended pacing, moving in and out of Tourmaline's keyhole-shaped view and leaving her with only Professor Sharma to look at. His robes were voluminous on his scarecrow frame, and his thick, black brows were stuck at their customary anxious tilt. The younger professor wrung his hands. "But what are we going to do about it? We have to *do* something."

By this time Tourmaline was thoroughly curious about who or what it was that had gone missing, and impatient to find out. She ran through a mental inventory of items that she'd recently repurposed from various locations around the university (most recently a glass paperweight with a dandelion clock suspended inside it; she wanted to investigate how the flower had managed to get in there in the first place).

"You forget yourself, Professor Sharma," said Aladeus

sharply. His tone pulled Tourmaline away from musing on her own thievery. She felt a surge of kinship and sympathy for the younger professor, having been on the receiving end of Aladeus's frosty disdain more times than she cared to remember.

"Persephone is a valuable asset to Pellavere University and no one knows that better than I. But there's simply no point sending anyone after her. We have no idea where she was."

Tourmaline took in a sharp breath before she could help it, and then held it. But the professors didn't notice. They carried on talking, though Tourmaline's wits were scattered and she was only half listening. *Persephone* had disappeared? Tourmaline's whole body felt strange and prickly. Her mother. Her mother, who had been on one of her archaeological digs finding artefacts for the great museum at the university, had vanished?

She let out her breath slowly and pressed her widened eye firmly to the keyhole, listening especially carefully, just as Professor Aladeus said, in a much kinder voice, "If this had only happened while Persephone was on one of her more usual missions ... but it didn't. Regrettable, of course, but there's really nothing we can do."

"Yes, of course," Professor Sharma agreed, sounding less sure. "You wouldn't think it mattered what she was hunting for. But maybe it does after all, and given the delicate nature of the task she was undertaking… I mean, was there ever really any source after all? I for one was never certain."

Tourmaline wished that the professor would do a lot more explaining and a lot more of finishing his own sentences than he was currently doing. She strained her ears for the response.

Professor Aladeus made a sound of agreement. Tourmaline held her breath again. She didn't know exactly what the professors were talking about, but Persephone had worked for the university Tourmaline's entire life. She'd always hunted artefacts. That was what she did. It was *all* that she did. It wasn't possible that she'd gone off to do something else and not even told her own daughter.

Tourmaline tried very hard to keep a sense of panic that she could feel somewhere in her feet from rising any higher. She didn't like to think what it might do if it reached an important part like her stomach.

"Perhaps," Professor Sharma suggested, "she shouldn't have gone at all?"

"Oh, but there's no stopping Persephone when she has a mind to do something," said Professor Aladeus. He said it as though having a mind was distasteful.

"Quite," said Professor Sharma. "Even so, if we're never going to be able to replenish the source…" He tailed off, wrung his hands again and blinked several times. He seemed to be waiting for Professor Aladeus to present some solution to this mystifying problem. Then he suddenly seemed to be struck by a completely different idea. "What of the child?"

Tourmaline shifted further forwards, pressing against the doors of the magician's box.

Professor Aladeus's expression took on a disagreeable long-suffering air. There followed a list of general complaints about her, ranging from eavesdropping, which Tourmaline could hardly deny given her current situation, to greed when it came to pudding, at which Tourmaline bristled.

"I see," said Professor Sharma faintly, when Professor

Aladeus had finished, "but surely she needs to be told about the current development regarding her mother?"

"Yes, yes," said Professor Aladeus impatiently. "I'll deal with it presently. Perhaps a part-time job in the university grounds might correct her failings. Or maybe a position in the military?"

Tourmaline blinked in outrage several times. Both of those options amounted to orders being given and followed and Tourmaline had no interest in that.

Aladeus consulted his pocket watch and sighed. "In fact, I'll deal with Tourmaline now. Come, Professor Sharma."

Professor Aladeus swept out of the room and Professor Sharma hastened to follow. Tourmaline paused for a second, letting the shock of what she had just heard sink in, and then she pushed at the false back of the magician's box, squeezed into the space-between and scrambled to where she should have been in the first place.

When she reached the music room, she exited the space-between via a large urn outside the room and burst through the door to face George, who let out a startled squeak on his euphonium.

She rushed over to the harpsichord and launched into a rendition of the university's anthem that was loud and enthusiastic more than it was accurate.

George opened his mouth to say something, just as Tourmaline noticed with dismay that Mai had come into the music room at some point during her absence. Then the door swung open. Professor Aladeus stood on the other side, short, severe, and already frowning. Professor Sharma shifted anxiously behind him.

Tourmaline blew her curls out of her eyes, rallied her playing and turned the page on the score in front of her, more for effect than anything else. She kept playing right up until Professor Aladeus cleared his throat loudly, when she broke off.

He looked at her over the top of his spectacles, his spectacular eyebrows lowering, and she looked back, hazel eyes wide.

"You appear to be out of breath, Tourmaline."

"Do I?" she asked.

His eyebrows sank to dangerous depths. "A word, if you can spare the time from your studies."

His tone made it sound like this was the last thing he wanted to do, at the same time as implying that Tourmaline's efforts weren't worthy of the word "studies". Then he turned on his heel, his robes flapping like a raven's wings. Tourmaline scrambled out of her seat to follow him.

She cast a glance back, first at George, whose dark eyes were round with fear on her behalf, and then at Mai, whose shrewd brown ones were contemptuously curious. Thankfully she'd chosen to say nothing instead of telling on Tourmaline.

Behind Mai, hanging on the wall, was an imposing painting of the current dean of Pellavere University, who was also George's mother. She stood looking down on the classroom, and on Tourmaline, a bookcase at her back and a black-and-white cat at her feet. She did not look very forgiving.

George and Tourmaline had been friends for as long as Tourmaline could remember and even before that too, if Josie was to be believed. He was the exact same height as Tourmaline herself, which was to say quite short, but he was slighter, with pale skin and straight, brown hair. He, like Tourmaline, had spent his whole life at the university, though he'd made rather less free use of the space-between due to a proper fear and respect of the rules that Tourmaline herself had never been able to master.

Mai, on the other hand, had only been at the university since the beginning of the term a few weeks ago when her mother had joined the faculty in an administrative role. She was taller than any twelve-year-old had a right to be, with straight, jet-black hair and light brown skin. Tourmaline had regarded her with the suspicion she felt for all new things. Her first impression hadn't been favourable. Mai seemed aloof and said little in the classes the three now had together, and Tourmaline would have been quite happy if she'd never turned up, leaving herself and George to continue as they always had.

The door swung shut and Professor Aladeus strode off down the corridor past several marble busts of former professors, who seemed to be frowning down at Tourmaline as she ran to keep up.

"We'll use your study, shall we?" said Professor

Aladeus, not waiting for Professor Sharma to answer before he turned abruptly and swung open a door, causing several sheets of paper to launch themselves from a desk and scatter on the floor.

The name plate on the door had still not been etched properly, so Professor Sharma had tacked up a handwritten placard that made Tourmaline feel much better about her own terrible handwriting. Professor Aladeus sat behind the desk, leaving Professor Sharma to loiter awkwardly by the tiny window while Tourmaline herself squeezed in and tried to close the door. The study was little more than a box room, or perhaps a repurposed store cupboard.

"So," said Professor Aladeus briskly.

Tourmaline tried to compose her face into innocence, though her palms were a little sweaty. She wiped them on her trousers and Professor Aladeus closed his eyes for a brief moment of disapproval.

"I'm afraid we have some bad news," said the professor.

"Oh dear," said Tourmaline.

Aladeus frowned. "Yes, well. No use in sugar-coating it.

Your mother, I'm sorry to say, appears to have gone missing. But do rest assured, dear child, that the university won't stop until we've unearthed her again." He paused and seemed to ponder the unsuitability of suggesting that Persephone was in need of "unearthing". "That is to say, we'll use every means at our disposal to find her again, so chin up, no need to make a fuss, and so on and so forth."

He nodded, as if satisfied that he'd dealt with the situation. Tourmaline found that she didn't have to pretend to be worried or upset because she suddenly and very much felt both. Obviously the university had no real intention of finding her mother.

She took a step forwards and bumped into Professor Sharma's desk. "What do you mean, missing?"

Professor Aladeus looked as though he hadn't been expecting questions and was quite put out by this one. "Exactly that, my dear. Missing. Vanished. Gone."

"But how is that possible? I mean, wasn't she on an archaeological dig for the university? How can she simply have vanished? How can the university not know where she is?"

Professor Aladeus shook his head as if this was all

getting out of hand now and he'd rather see an end to it. He gestured in the air. "Well, you know Persephone, always going off on some whim or other. We can't be expected to—"

"My mother," interrupted Tourmaline, "does not go off on whims. She uses empirical evidence and meticulous research methods and – and—"

"Yes, of course," said Professor Sharma. Tourmaline was glad he'd gathered up the courage to interrupt since she'd forgotten everything else her mother had told her about what she did.

Professor Sharma glanced nervously at Professor Aladeus and then back to Tourmaline. "Your mother is a remarkable scholar and an intrepid archaeologist." Here he seemed to run out of steam and visibly wilted under the continued glare of Professor Aladeus.

"As I was saying," said Aladeus, "I daresay it's nothing to worry about. The dean has been fully appraised of the situation and she knows that Persephone is a resourceful woman who will undoubtedly make it back. Now off you go." He looked down at the desk, adjusted his spectacles and pretended to be engrossed in a research paper that Tourmaline was absolutely certain he had no interest in since it wasn't even his desk. She looked to Professor Sharma, who suddenly became fascinated by a spot on the wall some two feet above her head.

Tourmaline clamped her mouth shut and left the room with her fists clenched.

They were both liars.

But what was she going to do about it?

Chapter Two

"Aladeus didn't even bother to invite me into his own study," said Tourmaline, hurling her shoe on to the floor. It had been as though she wasn't worth the trouble.

"You do tend to steal from him," said George mildly, laying his book down on the arm of the chair. He could tell he wasn't going to be allowed to finish his chapter, which was a shame because the heroine of the story was just about to stand up to her overbearing mother for the first time and George was particularly looking forward to that.

Tourmaline took the ancient-looking coin she'd borrowed from Professor Sharma's desk from one of her many pockets and sighed as she rolled it between her finger and thumb. She'd come into the little sitting room that she shared with George and told him almost everything that had happened – the conversation she'd overheard in the magician's box (the important part about her mother being missing, not the incomprehensible part about Persephone keeping things from her – she wasn't ready to talk about that yet), her hurried exit through the space-between, and then the outrageous lies she'd just been told. And though there was a cheerful fire in the hearth, Tourmaline was now in a foul mood. She didn't want to admit it but she was more than a little worried about her mother.

George eyed the coin glinting in the firelight but didn't say anything. He didn't approve of Tourmaline's tendency to collect other people's shiny belongings like a magpie. But he was secretly a little bit awed by how she could do such things without it seeming to worry her at all. His stomach was in knots just thinking about it.

"I have to make them find her, George. What am I going to do?" Tourmaline threw her other shoe in a different direction from the first.

George considered. He didn't think there was

anything Tourmaline *could* do but he knew better than to say so and he really did want to help. "Maybe you could talk to Professor Sharma when Professor Aladeus isn't there? You did say he thought the university should do something. He might help."

Tourmaline snorted. "Aladeus won't let him. He can't even stand up for himself, so how's he going to stand up for my mother?" Her earlier sympathy with Professor Sharma had evaporated as she'd stalked along the corridors back to her and George's small corner of the sprawling university.

George winced slightly at Tourmaline not using the title "Professor".

"Well, then perhaps you could go to my mother?" He hadn't really wanted to suggest it, mainly because he thought Tourmaline would ask *him* to do it instead and he suspected he was more intimidated by his own mother than Tourmaline was. But as dean of the university, if anybody could find out where Persephone had gone, his mother could.

Tourmaline immediately brightened, stuffing Professor Sharma's coin back into one of her pockets.

Then she paused and stared pensively at the fire for a second. "There must be a reason Aladeus didn't tell me the truth, though. We'll have to be careful."

George nodded. Asking anything of his mother required great care, and ideally one would have a clear line of exit from her presence.

He glanced at his book. "Sometimes adults think children can't understand the truth. They think it's better to come up with some other version of the facts."

His friend dropped into her chair, which was opposite George's. "You're right. Adults never answer a question properly, do they? They always have some reason they don't want to tell you the truth but even then you can't say they're lying. They *really* don't like that. I don't know why they can't just speak plainly."

George was pretty sure his mother said everything very plainly. Maybe even too plainly.

Tourmaline crossed her legs underneath herself on her chair and leaned forwards. "We can't just go to her demanding she save my mother. It'll be best if she thinks it's her own idea to send a rescue party rather than ours. She'll like that better."

George couldn't argue with that since it was entirely true.

"First," said Tourmaline, leaning so far off her chair she was balancing right on the edge, "we start talking about how fantastic the museum is and how clever your mother is for collecting all the old junk—"

"Artefacts," said George, but Tourmaline barely paused.

"Right, the old junk artefacts, and *then* we move on to the latest dig site and we ask where it is—"

"You don't even know where Persephone was before she went missing?" said a voice from the back of the room.

George let out a little squeak. Neither he nor Tourmaline had realized Mai was in the room, but there she was, curled into a high-backed winged chair that had been turned to face away from the fire. Mai stood up from the shadows and looked down at both of them. "If you don't know where she was before she went missing, how can you possibly hope to find out where she is now?"

George glanced at Tourmaline to confirm that she

was wearing the scowl that Mai always brought out. She was.

Mai either didn't notice or didn't care. "And what exactly *are* artefacts? My mother hasn't mentioned them at all."

"Oh," said George, who was always ready to talk about this subject. "That's probably because she isn't in the archaeology department. They're priceless objects, and Tourmaline's mother is the most famous artefact hunter in Escea. No, not just Escea, probably the whole world. She's one of the reasons that Pellavere University is the best in the country. All the students want to come here. There are lots of other hunters, but none of them are *real* hunters. Persephone Grey is the only one sanctioned by our university; the others are a bunch of crooks and rogues."

Mai frowned. "Why is Persephone a hunter and the others are crooks and rogues? Don't they do the same thing?"

George didn't even pause to answer the question. "She's been to jungles and up mountains and down ice crevasses to seek things out for the university museum.

Anyway, the artefacts could be a jewelled headdress worn by an ancient queen, or an arrowhead from the War of the Tributaries, or a piece of parchment from the Scrolls of Nevarsi. They can come from any period in history, really. In the museum the displays are divided up by age. There's the Age of Queens and the Age of Marble, and the—"

"And another thing," said Mai, turning away from George. "What's the space-between? And does Professor Aladeus really have a magician's disappearing box in his study? What do you think he uses it for?"

In the silence that followed, one of the logs on the fire popped while George nursed his hurt feelings and Tourmaline realized that Mai now knew about several things she hadn't before, including the space-between.

Tourmaline said, in her chilliest tone, "Why were *you* listening to my and George's private conversation?"

Mai (who had more questions about the dubious nature of collecting artefacts but also wanted to remind Tourmaline that she was perfectly entitled to be in the room and couldn't help it if they hadn't bothered to notice her) opened her mouth to retort. George braced himself, but Tourmaline abruptly stood up. "Come along, George," she said. "Let's get ready."

"Ready for…?"

Tourmaline cast a mutinous glance at him.

"Right." He hastily stuffed his book under his arm and followed her out of the room. If Tourmaline was on the warpath, he definitely needed to be by her side. By her side and maybe a little bit behind her, though, if she was going to talk to the dean.

"Are – are we going to talk to my mother?" he asked, trotting a little to keep up with Tourmaline. "Do – do you think we should perhaps prepare a little better first?" He looked down at Tourmaline's current attire. Her trousers were dusty along the shins and knees and there was a stripe of chalk on the waistband.

She paused to pick at a lunch-time stain that might have been egg, or custard, or both, and sighed.

"You know how she feels about untidiness," said George. "Especially at dinner time."

"You're right," said Tourmaline. "You'd better get cleaned up. I'll meet you outside the Great Hall."

She strode off towards her own room.

"You are going to get cleaned up too, aren't you?"

"Yes!" Tourmaline called back. "And hurry up! Don't take forever to get ready."

George opened his mouth indignantly but then thought better of speaking. He ran off to his own little bedroom, which was in another, far grander wing of the university residence next to his mother's suite.

Tourmaline charged up the twisting stone stairs to find that her room was not empty. It was full of someone who was fishing through a pile of Tourmaline's belongings, which may or may not have started life belonging to other people.

"There you are," said Josie. She was a little older than Persephone, perhaps even forty, with warm, golden-brown skin and hazel eyes more on the green side than Tourmaline's. Eyes which now clamped a determined gaze on Tourmaline. "I'm returning this –" she shook a jar of semi-precious stones and minerals – "to the Geology department and I don't want to hear one single word about it."

"Fine," said Tourmaline. She had already flung off her jacket and yanked her wardrobe doors open. Now she was pulling various pairs of trousers from their hangers.

"Not that I'm not very, *very* happy about this strange new turn of events," said Josie, "but why exactly are we looking for clean clothes?"

"No particular reason," said Tourmaline, in a tone that told Josie there was a very particular reason but if she wanted to know it, she'd have to find out some other way. "Should I wear these?" She held up a pair of smart, blue, multi-pocketed trousers. "They match with this." She yanked out a matching jacket with braiding and twisted buttons.

Josie decided to put her suspicions where she could snatch them back up at a moment's notice and take Tourmaline's baffling new interest in her own appearance as a gift.

"Perfect," she said. Tourmaline beamed, hurriedly pulled on the clothes, and was in her dressing-table chair before Josie could arm herself with a silver hairbrush.

"Hair?" Josie enquired cautiously.

Tourmaline's gaze roved for a second before it landed on a photograph tacked to the side of the mirror. "Like that," she said, looking up at Josie, who was now standing behind her. "Exactly like that."

Josie nodded and got to work. It wouldn't take long. The photograph was of Tourmaline's mother, and mother and daughter had exactly the same shoulder-length hair with tight, springing coils. But where Persephone's hair was black and her skin tanned, Tourmaline's curls and skin were several shades lighter.

In the photograph, Persephone was standing with her head held proudly, hair slicked back and one foot planted on a rock overlooking a sweeping view of the Valley of Queens. It looked so different to Escea. Not that Tourmaline even knew what all of Escea was like. She herself had never been anywhere except the university and into Brenia City a few times. Persephone had travelled practically the whole world, and Tourmaline longed to do the same and more.

She stared at the likeness of her mother as Josie tugged and smoothed her hair into place and used a million clips to pin back the curls. Hair was where the similarities between mother and daughter both started and stopped. Nothing else about Tourmaline, from her height (middling as yet, but still taller than Persephone), to the colour of her eyes (hazel where Persephone's were dark brown), to the many freckles on her skin, was anything like her mother.

Persephone was short and strong, with a capable, adventurous air about her. She was very clever and knew a great deal about history and geography, and how to travel from the snow-covered mountains of Aerith to the luminous caverns of Zhenzhing without losing her compass or contracting an infectious disease. She knew how to get a drink from the inside of a Yakosh tree, and she had once told Tourmaline a story about a daring escape from a booby-trapped tomb guarded by a secret society of women defending the treasure inside. Tourmaline thought that the women might have had a point, but the story had been very exciting anyway.

"There," said Josie, admiring her work on Tourmaline's hair. "Exactly the same."

Tourmaline scrutinized her reflection. The hair was good, but she looked exactly nothing like Persephone otherwise.

"Do you think I look like my father?" she asked Josie.

Josie put her hands on Tourmaline's shoulders and regarded her firmly in the mirror. "You look like yourself."

Tourmaline frowned. She didn't know who her father was, and by extension she often couldn't be sure who she herself was. She thought that it might be nice to know, but unfortunately her father was even more of a mystery than her mother.

Tourmaline had no doubt that Persephone loved her, but if Tourmaline herself was, as Josie liked to say, an open book, then Persephone was very much a closed one. Tourmaline might go as far as to say that she was also locked, heavily guarded and possibly glued shut.

"Where did my mother meet him?" she asked, hoping if she came at the subject a little sideways, she might get some actual information.

"It's of no significance who he was or where he came from and you know it, Tourmaline," Josie said severely. Tourmaline paid her no mind. Josie had a lot to say about a great many subjects, from the state of gentlemen's fashion these days to the latest theories about quantum physics, and all of it was invariably severe. But Josie had been there ever since Tourmaline could remember – employed initially as a nanny for George, a job which soon expanded to include Tourmaline and after that to include the general herding, teaching, entertainment and despairing that came with her.

Josie gave Tourmaline a brief but very firm hug. "Now, are you going to tell me why we just spent time making you look fit for an important interview?"

She eyed Tourmaline shrewdly. Tourmaline smiled sweetly. Josie was undoubtedly one of the best adults to ever have existed, but she was still just an adult, and as such, couldn't fully be trusted not to stop Tourmaline interrupting the dean's dinner in the way she intended.

Ten minutes later, Tourmaline was striding towards the doors of the Great Hall with her heart and mind set on one very specific goal. She was going to make the university find her mother.

Chapter Three

George hurried to keep up with Tourmaline, his shiny shoes pattering on the polished wood floor.

"Slow down!" He was half afraid that Tourmaline's velocity would propel her straight into his mother, who was probably captivating her dinner guests at this point. George hadn't a clue who that might include, only who it definitely did not include – namely himself and Tourmaline.

His friend reached for the brass handle of the imposing door to the Great Hall.

"Tourmaline, stop!" said George, getting braver in his desperation.

Tourmaline heard something in his voice that made her pause and stop. Not that George knew quite what he was going to say next. He blinked at his friend.

"I think we need to consider a plan of attack. You know, *before*, you actually attack. Mai interrupted us and I'm not sure—"

"I know, George, and usually I'd say you're right, because you usually are, but there isn't time. My mother is missing and every second could be vital." Tourmaline sighed. "I'm sorry but we just have to do this. Imagine if it was *your* mother who'd vanished. Wouldn't you want me to do everything I could to help?"

George's chin retracted almost to his bow tie as he thought about this and found he couldn't wrap his mind around what it would be like if his mother suddenly vanished. It left him feeling uncomfortably disloyal for a second before somebody opened the door from the other side and saved him the trouble of answering Tourmaline's question.

The man who had opened the door was the head of the History department, a tall, broad, imposingly handsome figure named Professor Swanson. He was also known, and had been for the last twelve months, as George's stepfather, Jacoby.

"Hello!" said his stepfather, looking, as he always did, pleased but mildly nervous to see George.

George, who hadn't the slightest idea how he could make anyone nervous and was much more used to being nervous himself, swallowed, smiled and blinked.

"Hello, Jacoby."

Jacoby stepped out of the hall, bringing with him the tinkle of glasses and cutlery, very refined voices saying very clever things, and very polite laughter. He looked between George and Tourmaline, a flicker of startled approval crossing his face as he took in Tourmaline's flawless outfit.

"May I ask what you're both doing here? By the way, wonderful essay you turned in to Professor Aladeus last week."

George stared up at his stepfather, his eyes wide. Professor Aladeus had been charged with the history education of the children, which had not improved his temper or his feelings towards them. George had never dreamed that anyone other than Professor Aladeus would be interested in his history essays (and even then, he doubted there was a great deal of interest).

"Thank you," he said faintly.

"You have a very keen understanding of the subject," said Jacoby.

Still blinking in shock, George nodded and tried to catch a glimpse of Tourmaline. She had steamed off ahead into the Great Hall and was making a beeline for the dean, who was seated at the head of the dining table.

"Oh dear," he said, hurrying after his friend with an apologetic glance at his stepfather.

The hall was laid out for an intimate dinner with the dean's favoured members of the faculty, with rows of fine china, dazzling crystal glasses and silverware polished to a high shine. Wall sconces held huge light bulbs which sent a soft yellow glow across the scene of professors as servants glided around with silver platters holding bubbling glasses of wine.

Jacoby hurried after George, who was trying not to run – it would only make things worse. "I have some books you may be interested in," said Jacoby, pulling George's attention back to the conversation. "I'd be very happy to lend them to you, if you'd like?"

George's polite smile, as he looked up at his

stepfather, expanded to something much more like his actual smile.

"I'd like that very much," he said, and he found that he was looking forward to it, and maybe even to discussing the books after he'd read them. Then he broke into a walk so fast that it could easily have been mistaken for running because the guests, and the dean herself, had noticed Tourmaline. The dean stood up with a look that very clearly said "What is the meaning of this?", which she directed first at Jacoby, then George, then Tourmaline herself.

George caught up with his friend, wrestling his waistcoat back into place just as Tourmaline, in her politest voice, said, "Excuse me."

Faiza Gramercy, Head of Artefacts, dean of the university, holder of no less than four postgraduate degrees, and also George's mother, looked down.

"Tourmaline."

Tourmaline was only slightly daunted. "I've come to ask you about my mother."

Professor Aladeus cleared his throat. He had been sitting right next to the dean, Tourmaline noticed with a frown. The dean gracefully sank back into her seat. The professor said several things that Tourmaline couldn't hear into the dean's ear, and they both glanced at her.

Dean Gramercy's face became a picture of concern as she turned back to Tourmaline. "Oh, my dear, dear girl. So dreadful, but rest assured, if anyone can find their way back to us, Persephone can. And of course, we're doing everything we can to locate her. Professor Aladeus has spoken to you about the matter already, I believe?"

Tourmaline squirmed. "Yes, but—" She looked at Professor Aladeus. He had assumed an air of grave but condescending concern. She wanted to say that she knew for a fact that the university was doing precisely nothing to find her mother, but she couldn't exactly reveal how she knew that. Not without giving away the secret of the space-between and letting everyone know that she had been spying and eavesdropping.

The dean smiled the sort of smile that meant she was dismissing Tourmaline. "And of course, this really isn't the time or place."

"No, of course," said Tourmaline, "but…"

"But?" asked the dean. She was starting to sound a little frayed.

"But who is looking for her?" asked Tourmaline. "Where have they gone?

"Tourmaline," said Dean Gramercy, and her tone this time had George shrinking and tugging on Tourmaline's sleeve. "Professor Aladeus has assured me that there's nothing to worry about. Everything that can be done is being done, and I'm sure Persephone will return, perhaps even before the search party do. Ah, the first course is here."

The dean turned back to Professor Aladeus before Tourmaline could say anything else. But Tourmaline was not easily deterred and her gaze swept the room for another target, alighting on Professor Sharma. He had just returned from the bathroom, and when he saw her promptly fled in the opposite direction.

Tourmaline looked at George, whose eyes pleaded with her as he tilted his head towards the door. She scowled and marched away from the dean, down the length of the table, stopping only to cram a liberal handful of soft, warm rolls into one of her pockets.

"But there isn't a search party," George whispered, with a fearful glance back as they left the hall. "Is – is Professor Aladeus lying to my mother too?"

"I told you he was!" Tourmaline bit savagely into a roll and strode off down a corridor. "He's never liked me and he's never liked my mother. He probably wants her job for himself."

"Where are we going?" asked George.

"To the Stables," said Tourmaline. "Your mother said they're doing everything they can to find *my* mother and I don't believe it, but I need to be certain. If they sent anyone to find her, then that someone would have been travelling in some*thing*. I want to see if anything's missing from the Stables."

George nodded and picked up the pace. "If there is, that might also give us a clue to where Persephone was, before she disappeared."

"How?" asked Tourmaline.

"Well, there'd be no point taking an ice-sled to a desert."

"I hadn't thought of that," said Tourmaline and she squeezed George's arm to show him she was pleased.

42

She thought about telling him that Persephone hadn't even been hunting for an artefact and that something at the university needed replenishing, but she wasn't sure what any of it meant. And the thought of admitting that her mother had been keeping things from her made her neck feel hot and itchy.

They hurried down the dusty stone corridors, past spiral staircases leading up to forgotten turrets, out through the kitchen gardens (it was starting to get dark now) and on to the Stables. No one was around, either having been invited to the dinner or dining elsewhere, and Tourmaline made short work of the nutlock. The nutlock was something like a padlock, shaped like an acorn with a tiny twisting mechanism inside it that was supposed to be next to impossible to crack, but which hadn't been designed with a determined twelve-year-old girl in mind.

George glanced around, trying not to hop from one foot to the other, and then the doors were open and the two of them stepped inside on to the mezzanine gallery that ran around the inside wall of the building.

Below them, carved into the ground, lay a

subterranean level. The Stables was home to every mode of transport available: vast hot-air balloons bobbing under the cavernous roof, ready to be released at a moment's notice; carriages, canoes, light aircraft, automobiles… In short, everything but horses, which were kept elsewhere.

Each station had a motorcycle or a coracle or a sled. As Tourmaline frowned and gazed down the length of the Stables (it was quite lengthy), George said, "There's nothing missing."

"Nothing at all," said Tourmaline, raising her eyebrows and pursing her lips. She'd suspected as much but seeing the proof was still difficult.

George's eyebrows almost met in the middle. "What are you thinking?"

Tourmaline's pinched face pinched even further. She decided she should probably tell George a bit more of what she'd overheard. He really was very clever. "My mother isn't even looking for an artefact, she's looking for sauce."

"What?"

"The professors said so. Sauce? *The* Sauce?"

44

George frowned. "Are you sure about that?"

"I know what I heard," said Tourmaline peevishly. "Or maybe it was source." She wrote the two words in the air to show George and sighed. "I still don't know what it is, though."

George shook his head. "Neither do I."

"What are you doing?" The voice came from behind them and George and Tourmaline both jumped. George's hand fluttered over his heart and Tourmaline scowled.

"I saw you leave the hall," said Mai. "I mean, after I followed you there. What's all this about a source?"

"Nothing," said Tourmaline, at the same time as George said, "We don't know."

"Are you going to find your mother?" asked Mai, her eyes narrowing.

"None of your business," said Tourmaline, at the same time as George said, "We're trying to."

"So what's this source got to do with it?" asked Mai.

George began an answer based on some ideas he had, but Tourmaline wasn't fully listening. She was suddenly busy thinking about the last time she had spoken to her mother. Tourmaline had not been gracious. Not gracious at all. In fact, she'd been downright rude.

"Where are you going this time?" Tourmaline had asked, seeing through Persephone's open bedroom door that she was packing again. Persephone looked slightly flushed and hectic, as she tended to when she was about to leave. Usually, she would stop, though, and tell Tourmaline that she was going to find the Heart of Sublantia or seek out a new lead on an artefact in the mountain caves of Vilok. This time, she hadn't. She hadn't even answered Tourmaline properly, just rather curtly said something about an island.

"*Fine,*" Tourmaline had said. "*Don't* tell me, then. I don't care anyway." And she'd strode off.

What if Persephone never came back? The last thing she ever said to her mother would forever and always be that she didn't care. But she did. She cared so much it made her fingertips cold and her chest tight.

She crossed her arms, put her hands under her armpits, and squeezed herself.

"How are we going to find out?" asked Mai.

"Find out what?" said Tourmaline.

"Where she's gone and what this source thing is?" said Mai a little impatiently.

"I'm not sure."

"I have an idea," said George, then instantly seemed to regret speaking. "Except it's something we shouldn't do. In fact, it's a bit … we're definitely not allowed."

Tourmaline was thoroughly intrigued and already fully on board.

Mai shrugged. "I suppose you really can't do anything about it, then."

"She's probably right," said George reluctantly.

Tourmaline looked at her friend and quietly realized, with a sense of inevitability, that it was up to her to save her mother.

"George," she said. "Tell me your idea."

George's face blanched slightly. "We could… I mean, we shouldn't, but… I think it might be useful if…"

"George!"

George's shoulders slumped. "We could break into Persephone's lab."

Chapter
Four

George blinked tiredly at Tourmaline and Mai after their classes the next day. Keeping his eyes open in the stuffy classroom during mathematics had been a battle that he hadn't entirely won, and now he was feeling a bit dazed.

"George?" said Tourmaline. She shaded her eyes from the late-afternoon sun that was coming through the branches of the apple trees. They were sitting on the grass outside Persephone's lab and though it made Mai's eyes itch, she and Tourmaline still didn't look anywhere near as bad as George felt. Staying up past 10 p.m. after their trip to the Stables had been exciting, but not something he wanted to repeat any time soon.

"George!" Tourmaline shook his arm.

"Sorry. I'm not sure it's possible," he said.

The lab was behind the museum and the only way into it was *through* the museum. After an incident involving Tourmaline and a priceless vase the children were barred from entering the museum, and since it was currently closed anyway, Tourmaline had decided that they should climb in through one of the windows.

The problem with this was that the windows were small and circular and set high up in the walls to protect the privacy of the archaeologist inside and the secrecy of what she was doing. And probably to prevent break-ins like the one that was about to happen if Tourmaline had her way, George thought to himself.

"I know the ladder is a little short," Tourmaline conceded.

George looked at the ladder (one they'd borrowed from the orchardist, and which she used for pruning and tending to the trees they were sitting beneath), then squinted at the building.

"Two feet too short," he said. "Approximately."

"I could jump that," said Tourmaline. She moved to stand up and demonstrate and George pulled her back down in case they were seen.

"Not while balancing on a ladder you couldn't. And how are you going to get the window open? And how are you—"

"George, I don't want problems, I want solutions," said Tourmaline, who had been told the very same thing today in their mathematics lesson while George was trying to stay awake.

"I've got one," said Mai. "We can use a person to extend the ladder. Which, by the way, is why it's perfect there are three of us, but there's no need to thank me for coming."

This last remark was probably in response to Tourmaline's scowl when George had appeared to meet her with Mai in tow and she'd remembered that it wasn't just the two of them any more. She still wasn't sure she was happy about that fact.

Tourmaline plucked the head off a daisy. "What do you mean?"

"I mean," said Mai, "that if I climb the ladder, you could climb it and then climb *me* and reach the window."

"Sounds dangerous," said George, at the same time

as Tourmaline said, "Perfect."

George didn't much like it when he was overruled but since it happened quite often, he was at least used to it. He watched, and then decided not to watch, as Mai positioned the ladder, scaled it, and gestured to Tourmaline.

Tourmaline tried not to huff and puff, but it became impossible as she hauled herself past the other girl and in through the window.

"Are you coming?" Mai called down to George.

George shook his head. He wasn't sure his voice would come out right if he spoke.

Tourmaline appeared again at the window, leaned out and started pulling Mai up. Mai let out a colourful curse and then they were both gone, leaving George alone, loitering nervously and suspiciously by an open window and a stolen ladder.

Inside the lab, Tourmaline was balanced on top of a bookcase. Mai was next to her examining her own knee, which was bleeding after she'd scraped it on the bricks outside. She licked her fingers and pressed the spit on to the beads of blood.

Tourmaline was peering down at the lab, or what was left of it.

"It doesn't usually look like this, does it?" asked Mai.

Tourmaline shook her head. The lab had been ransacked, destroyed, torn apart. Someone had been looking for something. Someone who had been in a great hurry or very angry or both.

"I didn't think so," said Mai.

She sat on the bookcase and climbed down the shelves, wincing every time her knee bent. Tourmaline followed. She didn't say anything, so Mai picked her way across the mass of torn papers and cracked pottery on the floor to the desk, which was extremely large and solid and therefore still standing. There was an enticingly flat and clean piece of paper lying squarely on top of it. It was an advertisement of some kind, enthusiastic and brightly coloured, and it seemed to have escaped the devastation.

Mai picked it up and turned to show Tourmaline, treading on something that dug into her shoe. She bent to pick it up. "What's this?"

It was, or had once been, one of Persephone's tools,

but was now a mangled twist of metal.

Tourmaline's throat suddenly felt as though it was filled with clotted cream. Her eyes welled with tears, and she turned away to another bookcase. It had been pulled over, every single one of her mother's precious books discarded on the floor as though they meant nothing. Persephone would have been heartbroken and furious to see her lab like this.

Mai quietly shoved the paper into her pocket, turned in the opposite direction, and began pawing through a mound of what looked like dirt in a large tray.

Tourmaline was surprised to find that she needed a moment. She generally preferred to charge right in and maybe give whatever she was doing some thought later, if there was time. Right then, she found herself unable to do that.

She had only officially been in her mother's lab once before. Persephone had taken Tourmaline inside and let her admire and ask questions and even touch some of the artefacts she was currently studying and restoring. The artefacts themselves hadn't seemed all that interesting (they never were to Tourmaline), but

Persephone's excitement, her intense passion, had made an impression on Tourmaline. She remembered looking at her mother's animated face and feeling that she had, at last, been included in her mother's world. The fact that Persephone had allowed Tourmaline into the lab, invited her even? That had made it special. That had made her proud that her mother was so important. *That* had made the afternoon stick in her memory like nothing else ever had before or since.

The lab hadn't looked like it did now. The afternoon sun had been shining, warm and golden, through the circular windows. Tourmaline had been afraid to break the spell, afraid that Persephone would suddenly change her mind before she finally got to see what it was that kept her mother from her day and night.

Now she pushed her thumb into the middle of her chest and worked it around a bit to try to dislodge the way the memory made her happy and sad at the same time.

"What exactly are we looking for?" asked Mai.

Tourmaline jolted back to the task at hand. They'd better get on with it before anyone found them.

That wouldn't look good with the lab in the state it was in. She joined Mai, rifling through books and papers, pulling out desk drawers to find that they'd already been emptied, picking up smashed boxes and packing crates, rooting through the straw that had protected whatever precious artefacts had been inside.

This went on for some time in silence before Tourmaline stopped, feeling Mai's eyes on her for the third time.

"I hate to say it, but I don't think this is helping," said Mai.

Tourmaline's jaw clenched obstinately. "Just keep looking."

"We've already been in here a long time. And maybe whoever did this," Mai gestured to the chaos around them, "already took whatever it is that we're looking for."

"Then leave, if you want to," Tourmaline snapped. "I'm staying."

She was wondering if whoever had done this to the lab knew where Persephone was now. The thought of someone who was capable of doing this also finding her mother was horrible. She sat down on the floor facing her mother's desk, and more importantly, away from Mai, while she picked through some of the loose pages on the floor. Maybe there was some kind of code, or cipher, or note she could cleverly decode. She could hear Mai moving something behind her and she wished that George had come with her instead. *He* would never have expected her to give up. She purposely didn't think about the fact that George hadn't come at all.

That was when she saw something that she would never have seen if she hadn't been sitting on the floor. It was a piece of paper that had fallen behind her mother's desk and was now resting at an angle on the floor.

She scrambled forwards, wriggled under the desk, and gently eased the paper free.

"What is it?" asked Mai, her voice sharp with renewed interest.

"It's an excited note in my mother's handwriting," said Tourmaline, with just a hint of superiority in her tone. "And if I'm not mistaken, it's very important."

"How do you know?" Mai leaned over Tourmaline's shoulder, eager to see. "And what's an excited note?"

"Careful!" Tourmaline laid down the page, which had been torn from a notebook, and smoothed it over the desk.

"This is her excited writing," Tourmaline explained. "When she writes like this it means that she's made some kind of breakthrough in her research and she's very excited, which means that it's important."

"You mean when she scribbles?" asked Mai.

"My mother doesn't scribble," said Tourmaline with frosty dignity.

Mai ignored her and frowned at the note. "But what does it say?

Tourmaline squinted to see if it would help. "It says 'Consult the Living Archives' and then there are two question marks. Then underneath it says, 'Beware Evelyn Coltsbody', and after that there are three exclamation marks."

"That does sound important," Mai conceded, although she had no idea what it meant.

That was when they heard voices on the other side of the lab door.

Chapter Five

Mai's eyes darted up to the window. Tourmaline, who had more experience of being caught where she shouldn't be, shook her head frantically. There was no time to climb back up, and besides it would make too much noise.

She mouthed "hide" at Mai and dived under her mother's desk, cramming herself into the alcove in the middle. Mai flung herself into a pile of overalls and jackets that had been pulled from a coat stand and buried herself in the folds of material just as the door opened.

"This is Persephone Grey's lab," said a voice. A self-important voice that Tourmaline recognized immediately. Professor Aladeus. "Although I really don't think that anyone should be—"

"Thank you," said a cool, female voice. Two set of footsteps came in, then stopped.

"As you can see," said Professor Aladeus, "it's in quite a dreadful state. I doubt that anyone could find anything useful—"

"Thank you, Professor Aladeus," the other voice cut in again. "That will be all."

Tourmaline couldn't see the professor's face but she could just imagine his pompous, offended expression at someone speaking to him in this way. If she hadn't been so thoroughly frightened, she might have smiled.

A few seconds later, one set of footsteps walked away, and the woman continued further into the room. Tourmaline itched to move, to find a way to peep out and see who she was, but there was no way to do so without getting caught.

Several papers rustled. Shoes crunched on broken glass and Tourmaline winced. The woman sighed, paused, then quickly approached the desk. Too late, Tourmaline realized she'd left her mother's note right there, laid out in full view. But maybe it wouldn't mean

59

anything to this woman. Maybe she was looking for something else. Her footsteps stopped right in front of Tourmaline and a weight pressed down on the desk, making its joints creak slightly.

Something light hit the floor, very close to Tourmaline. Her eyes widened. It was a handkerchief. The embroidered kind that Tourmaline herself had, but never used (it was disgusting to use a handkerchief and then put it back in your pocket). The initials embroidered on to hers were T.G., but the initials on this particular handkerchief stopped the breath in her throat. They were *E.C.*

A hand reached down and scooped up the handkerchief. Then something rustled on the desk, the footsteps walked away and the door closed.

Tourmaline waited for a count of ten before she started to slowly squeeze back out from underneath the desk. Which was when she noticed that she'd been sitting right next to an entrance to the space-between. She stared at the wall and blinked several times, because the space-between was a hard thing to grasp no matter how many times she used it. It was definitely there but also not definitely there. A bit like a mirage, a bit like a dream, a bit like an idea that was too difficult to fully grasp, like long division, and that kept falling out of her head.

Nonetheless, there it was – an entrance, or exit, that she had never known existed, right inside her mother's lab. She moved towards it, consumed by curiosity. She felt the shift in the atmosphere that meant her head had broken through the thin barrier, and peered into the dim interior – an unfinished-looking place that didn't have any real substance that she could describe, but that existed regardless.

"Tourmaline?" The voice was small and muffled and coming from behind her, back out in the lab.

She shot a longing look at the space in front of her, wondered if she could come back later, then retracted herself first from the space-between and then from the space underneath the desk.

The woman who had been in the lab was gone, and so was the note.

"Mai?"

The pile of overalls and lab jackets in the corner

shifted, and Mai's face appeared. She looked as though she felt like Tourmaline herself had last week after eating too much cake, which was to say sick to her stomach.

Tourmaline helped her up and gave her a little shake. "Come on, we have to leave. Professor Aladeus could come back. Or that woman."

Mai's gaze snapped to her. "You don't know who that was?"

"I have a pretty good idea," said Tourmaline. "She dropped her handkerchief and I saw her initials."

Mai visibly swallowed.

"*E.C.*," said Tourmaline. "Evelyn Coltsbody!" She pulled Mai over to the bookcase and scrambled up. "Come *on*, Mai."

Outside, George had paced a line of grass entirely flat and he almost shouted when the two girls reappeared, clambering down the ladder. "Where have you *been*?"

"Only finding a brilliant clue *and* almost getting caught," said Tourmaline triumphantly. "Also? The orchardist is coming. Run."

Once they were seated in the refectory with steaming plates in front of them (after Josie had made them all wash twice and patched up Mai's knee) Tourmaline told George everything. She only embellished very slightly how close she was to being caught when Evelyn Coltsbody had dropped the handkerchief.

George eyed the students around them in the hall. Tourmaline was trying to keep her voice down. It didn't come naturally, but no one seemed to be paying the children any attention anyway.

"So Evelyn Coltsbody is trying to find your mother too?" asked George. "Is that why she took the notebook page? But then, she can't have had anything to do with Persephone going missing if she's trying to find her now. And she can't have destroyed the lab in the first place either."

Tourmaline shovelled another mouthful of steaming mashed potatoes into her mouth then immediately regretted it. She tried to chew while also blowing on the piping hot gravy inside her own mouth.

"Maybe E.C. isn't bad at all," said Mai, who had been very quiet since they'd left the lab and was now pushing her food in a slow circle around her plate. "Maybe she's trying to help Persephone."

Tourmaline snorted and then wished she hadn't. Some potato went down the wrong way and she had to cough for a full minute.

"I don't know," said George doubtfully when she'd finished. "Why did she steal our clue?"

"She didn't steal it," said Mai quickly.

George frowned.

Mai's gaze dropped to her plate. Her fork began to work faster. "What I mean is … she didn't know we wanted it. She didn't even know we were in the lab. So she didn't exactly steal it from us."

"She took something that didn't belong to her," said George, although he did glance a little guiltily at Tourmaline as he said it and wondered if it really did make someone a bad person if they were prone to taking things that weren't strictly theirs for the taking.

Tourmaline sighed. Her mouth was burnt and there was no denying it. "Look, none of that matters right now. What matters is that we find out where this Living Archive thing is so that we can find out where my mother went."

Mai looked from Tourmaline to George. "You don't know where it is?"

George looked apologetic. Tourmaline frowned.

By now George had thought of something else worrying. "Also, we need to be very careful Evelyn Coltsbody doesn't find us while we're doing it. I don't know who she is, but she sounds dangerous." He said the last word very quietly then glanced around as though the mysterious woman might be right behind him.

"OK," said Mai quickly. "Any ideas on how we find this place?"

Both girls looked at George, who paused. "Archives," he said. "Maybe they're part of the library?"

Tourmaline stood up abruptly and caught George's arm – he was just about to tuck into his cake and custard so she really had to pull – and the three children wove through the herd of students in the refectory on their way out.

"Do we have to go right now?" asked George, looking back regretfully at his cake.

"You can have cake afterwards," said Tourmaline firmly.

Ten minutes later they were standing in the very grand and very hushed library while Tourmaline stared up wide-eyed at the colourful stained-glass windows.

George nodded politely at a librarian he recognized. Then Tourmaline said, in a not-at-all hushed tone, "We're here to consult the Living Archives."

The librarian – a stocky young man with kind eyes and large muscles from carrying all those books – glanced quickly at the flagstones beneath their feet and turned a very odd shade that might have been called lilac.

"Please," said Tourmaline, thinking maybe librarians required politeness.

"I have no idea what you're talking about," said the librarian, making Tourmaline think that they were also terrible liars.

The librarian hurried away and Tourmaline, Mai and George turned to each other, forming a little huddle.

"I think," said Tourmaline, much more quietly, "that the Living Archives are supposed to be a secret."

"I bet Professor Aladeus knows where they are," said Mai.

Tourmaline snorted, in as muted a way as she could. "He's never going to tell us."

Mai frowned. "What about the other one you overheard talking?"

"Professor Sharma?" George said, so quietly the others could barely hear him. "I don't think he's going to tell Tourmaline either." He shrugged apologetically at his friend. There was no need, however, because Tourmaline had a small smile on her face.

"No, I don't think he would," she said, in a tone that made George wish she wasn't going to say whatever she was going to say next. "He might tell you, though."

"Oh," he said. "Oh, I—"

"You'll be fine," said Tourmaline, already striding out of the library. "Better than fine."

"Isn't it rather late?" said George desperately as they headed for Professor Sharma's study.

"It's barely seven thirty," said Mai.

"And we can't ask him tomorrow," said Tourmaline. "We have lessons all day."

"But what will I even say?" asked George, who could never believe the professors were just ordinary people like himself.

"George," said Tourmaline firmly. "You have an excellent vocabulary."

George blinked. That was true.

"You just need to put it to good use. And what better use than this? I *have* to find out where my mother went."

George nodded. This was also true.

"And if she consulted the Living Archives before she left, then that must be where she found out where to go, and if the librarian knows about the Living Archives then the professors must know too. We already decided that *I* can't ask Professor Sharma, and he doesn't even know Mai, so you see, George, it really has to be you. Good luck."

George had been nodding a little sadly the whole time Tourmaline was talking, and had almost resigned himself to the fact that Tourmaline was right, when he realized that they had reached Professor Sharma's study. And that Tourmaline had just knocked loudly on the door.

He made a small, startled noise as Tourmaline took a large step to the side of the door and pressed herself against the wall. Mai followed suit and the door opened.

Professor Sharma looked both anxious and harassed until he realized it was George.

"Oh, it's you," he said, visibly relieved. "Come in."

George threw a panicked glance at Tourmaline, who gave him her best, most encouraging smile. The professor stepped back, George followed him into the study, and the door closed.

"How can I help you?" asked the professor, who was very aware that George was the dean's son, and also very aware that the boy was in no way similar to the girl he sometimes had to deal with. That was a blessing and made him feel much more confident.

"I've come to— to ask you for some help with my studies," said George, and his voice only squeaked a little at the start.

"Really?" The professor leaned forwards, clearly pleased. "You have an interest in geography?"

"Oh, yes," said George.

"Because I have a text on oxbow lakes somewhere

69

here that is quite fascinating."

The professor began to cast about and then heaved a weighty tome on to the desk. A small puff of dust escaped and George coughed and wondered just how fascinating an oxbow lake could be.

"It's very detailed," said the professor, shunting it towards George.

"It looks riveting," said George, only feeling slightly guilty about the lie. "I was wondering if there's somewhere I could go to learn about the world, about specific … locations. Perhaps an archive?"

The professor's chin retracted nervously and George's followed suit all by itself.

"I don't think," said the professor, "that is to say, there isn't…"

George took three very quick, short breaths. "I am," he said, "George *Gramercy*, after all. I do know about the – the Living Archives."

The professor swallowed. "Yes, of course," he said.

"I would think," George said, "that if anyone is allowed to consult the Living Archives, it's me." It was the closest he had ever come to sounding haughty and it was making him feel quite sick. "So if you could kindly tell me where it is, I should be very grateful. I'm sure my mother—"

"Of course, of course," said the professor hastily. This was a new side to the boy that he hadn't experienced before or even dreamed existed and he wasn't enjoying how it made his face sweat.

George was feeling quite faint himself by this point, also never having dreamed that he would speak to a professor this way or that he would dare to bring his mother into such a conversation.

"I have a little – it's somewhere…" Professor Sharma hastily opened various drawers and emptied them on to his desk with increasing desperation until he finally found a small, unlabelled diagram.

"Here," he said, thrusting it at George.

George took the diagram and stood up abruptly. "Thank you so much," he said. "So sorry to have… Goodbye, Professor Sharma." He grabbed the doorknob and burst out into the corridor leaving the professor mopping himself with a handkerchief and wondering if he should have listened to his mother, who had warned him about the rigours of a life in academia.

George walked away on very uncertain legs, flanked by Tourmaline and Mai, who had appeared on either side of him the moment he stepped away from the door.

"George, you were brilliant," said Tourmaline, giving his arm, which hung limply at his side, a firm pat.

"I—" said George weakly.

"Don't worry, we were listening at the door," said Tourmaline. "We overheard everything." She took the diagram from George's hand and frowned at it.

"Is this a…" She turned the diagram round and when that made things no clearer, turned it over to look at the back.

"It's a sort of map," said Mai. "A blueprint, almost. The levels of the university are all on top of each other. I think this star is where the Archives are."

"Can you read it?" asked Tourmaline.

Mai looked around, frowned, and headed off down a darkened corridor, while Tourmaline looked at George in concern.

"Are you all right?" she asked, linking her arm with

his and towing him after Mai.

George shook his head. He wasn't sure quite who he was or if he'd ever be the same again.

Tourmaline dug around in her pockets and found a roll from the dean's interrupted dinner. It was flattened and a bit stale, but she dusted it off and handed it to George, who chewed on it absently, a little colour coming back into his cheeks.

"Tourmaline?" Mai had turned round and her face was lit up with a tense excitement that made Tourmaline squeeze George's arm tighter.

Mai brandished the diagram. "I know where the Living Archives are."

Chapter Six

"Are you sure you know where you're going?" asked Tourmaline tersely.

"You're just in a bad mood because you're nervous," said Mai helpfully.

They were already in a lower chamber of the university, chilly and all but abandoned. There was no turning back now.

"Maybe we should turn back," said George, his anxious whisper echoing strangely, his face lit eerily by the tallow lamp he was carrying. Tourmaline was used to George's second thoughts, along with his third and fourth, which were usually along the same lines.

She took hold of his hand and kept walking.

"You know, these archives must be very special if

they're such a secret," said Mai. "What do you think they'll be like?"

Tourmaline opened her mouth to give her opinion, thought about it for a second, and realized that she didn't actually have one since until this week she had never heard of the Living Archives and had no idea what they were. They were one more thing her mother had never told her about and she still didn't like the uncomfortable feeling of knowing her mother had so many secrets.

"George?" she said, with the air of someone handing over a question to a colleague because it was beneath her to answer.

George frowned. "I've been thinking," he said, "that it might be something to do with why our university is the best there is. I mean, the Living Archives must be a secret for a reason, and Pellavere must be the best for a reason, and so I thought that maybe the two were…" He trailed off, realizing he hadn't answered the question. "An archive is like a record or a collection, so maybe it's where all the knowledge in the university is stored."

"But isn't that just another library then?" asked Mai

as they passed by a heavy oak door.

"I don't think it can be," said George. "Otherwise it wouldn't be a secret."

"What, then?" asked Mai. "What's the point in all this knowledge if you aren't supposed to use it?"

George, who thought his evening had been quite trying enough already without this determined line of questioning, gave up entirely.

"So we could be walking into a room full of carnivorous books," said Mai, rather too cheerfully for George's liking.

"That would hardly be likely." Tourmaline had quietly been thinking about how many other things might have been kept from her, and whether she shouldn't devote more time to spying on people to remedy that. But now she glanced at George to confirm what she'd just said. His expression wasn't very reassuring.

"Or maybe it's a fountain of knowledge," said Mai, really gathering pace now. "I'm sure I read about that somewhere once. We should have bought swimsuits in case."

"I don't think it'll be a literal fountain," said George. He was wringing his hands.

"Talking owls!" said Mai. "Or unicorns! Are they wise? I think they must be. Maybe we'll have to drink potions and they could give us all the answers our hearts desire. Or they *could* be poison instead and we'd never know until—"

"Mai!" said Tourmaline, who hadn't known the other girl could be so imaginative. She had her arm round George's shoulder by this point and she could feel him quivering slightly.

"What?"

"I think we're here," said George faintly.

Mai consulted the diagram. "Oh," she said and even she sounded hushed.

They stood in front of towering arched doors flanked by stone pillars. Each door was carved with an intricate, minutely detailed pattern of leaves. Interspersed with the leaves were all manner of insects, crawling and wriggling and looping up and around and in between the leaves. Tourmaline noticed Mai shudder, though she tried to hide it.

On either side of the door, braziers hung from iron chains, casting flickering light over the children. George put his lamp on the floor. Tourmaline reached out a tentative hand. Her heart was beating uncomfortably, wondering what was on the other side of those doors. George told himself he was not, under any circumstances (except perhaps the carnivorous books thing being real) allowed to take a step back. Mai held her head up and assumed a disinterested air, while very firmly not looking at the mass of incredibly lifelike carved insects in front of her.

Tourmaline took hold of the iron ring (it was actually a snake, Mai noticed, with a barely suppressed shiver) and pulled.

Despite its height, the door glided open as though it weighed no more than a feather. George took a step back.

The avenue in front of them went on and on and on, straight as an arrow, until it disappeared into the distance. The light inside looked natural and when Tourmaline took a step forwards, almost compelled to get a closer look, she realized that the floor beneath her feet felt almost like earth.

None of them spoke as they stepped into the Living Archives and on to the ground that wasn't quite ground. On either side of the avenue stood trees, or they might have been the ends of bookcases. On closer inspection, it turned out they were both. There was something about them George felt but couldn't quite see. When he looked at them directly, they were trees – ancient and gnarled, their trunks and branches shaped in ways that seemed to confirm their tree-ness. But if he looked at them out of the corner of his eye, he could just about see the books, hidden between leaves, obscured by branches and part of them at the same time. It was more than a little confusing and he was glad that Tourmaline had dragged him away before pudding now that the archives seemed intent on making him feel sick.

Tourmaline looked one way and then the other, then turned round fast, hoping to catch whatever it was that was always just out of sight.

"This isn't – I don't know what's – can you see what—" Tourmaline stopped, realizing that she sounded, possibly for the first time in her life, like George.

"Never mind that. Look!" Mai pointed and all three of them looked.

The not-quite-forest whispered not-quite-words, and Tourmaline squinted to see if it would make any difference to the figures they were watching as they slowly moved in and out of the trees, or bookcases or whatever they were.

They looked not unlike the professors she was used to seeing in the levels of the university far above, except that they were older. Much older. Bent and stooped, shuffling and creaking.

"They're just *people*," whispered Mai.

"Yes," said George, with great relief.

"*You're* just a person," said a voice behind them. George clutched Tourmaline's arm as they all spun round.

"*I* am a Living Archive."

The Living Archive standing behind them was old, but *old* wasn't really an adequate description. She had skin like the bark of the trees that may or may not have been around them, and eyes so small they were barely visible. She was shorter than George and dressed in robes

80

that were either a greyish velvet, or very dusty, or both.

"*You're* the Living Archive?" said Tourmaline. She looked around at the other elderly figures. "*All* of you? But then what's this place?"

George gently elbowed Tourmaline to remind her about manners and respect and generally being intimidated by all adults and a vast number of other things.

The Living Archive looked offended and incredulous. "Only the backbone of this university, that's all," she said. "Only the reason that the professors know more than any faculty to ever exist. Only the reason that ground-breaking discoveries are made in our chemistry labs and new species of plants grow in our horticulture centre. That's all. But never mind being aware of the most important resource in the whole place, just barge in here and start asking pointless questions, why don't you."

"We're very sorry," said George, hastily. "We're sure the Living Archive is absolutely *essential*."

Mai nodded fervently as another Living Archive glowered at them while pushing a trolley full of books

...re student textbooks for an astrophysics ...y seemed to be a little bit damp.

"Excuse me," said Tourmaline, who did have manners but who chose to take shortcuts the vast majority of the time, "but I need to ask some questions."

The Living Archive looked at her.

"We thought this was the best place to come. Since you're so very clever," she added, hoping a bit of flattery would do the trick.

The Living Archive looked at her.

Tourmaline glanced at George, who nodded encouragingly. "We're in a hurry."

"Oh, well, in that case, if you're in a *hurry*, let me drop everything I was doing to assist you. It's not like this is the second time this week I've been pestered within an inch of my life. It's not like I was engaged in anything of particular importance," said the woman, who turned tail and stumped off surprisingly quickly down one of the aisles.

Mai and George looked at Tourmaline.

"Excuse me!" Tourmaline ran after the Living Archive and Mai and George ran after Tourmaline.

They all left the path and entered a part of the not-quite-forest that felt older and darker and altogether wilder and less civilized than it had before. George caught sight of a book that he thought looked interesting as he ran, but it covered itself in moss and seemed to slide back into the branches.

"Please wait!" Tourmaline called out. "I need to find my mother! Do you know where she is? She's gone missing and I think it's something to do with a source, or with Evelyn Coltsbody!"

The Living Archive stopped, turned round and hurried back. She peered at Tourmaline closely, pulled out a monocle that magnified her left eye so hugely Tourmaline could see each individual blood vessel in her eyeball, then peered at her some more.

"Who is your mother, child?"

"Persephone Grey," said Tourmaline, not sure what had brought about the sudden interest but very sure that she should use it to her advantage. "She disappeared and no one wants to do anything about it except that *I* do. But we don't know where to start because we don't know where my mother was before she went missing so it's pretty difficult to know where she might be now, and George said—"

"George?" The Living Archive swung her magnified eyeball in George's direction and scrutinized him from his boots to his brows.

"And who might you be?" she asked, continuing to Mai.

"Mai. My mother just started in the Department of—"

"I didn't ask who you are," snapped the Living Archive. "I asked who you might be."

Mai glanced at George, wide-eyed, and George shrugged, very carefully, so as not to redirect the Living Archive's attention to himself.

"Come with me." The Living Archive stomped off again down the aisle and Tourmaline found herself caught somewhere between a fast walk and a slow jog to keep up. Questions kept snapping at her tongue to get out but she held them back, which was not an easy task. She was afraid that the Living Archive would change her mind again and leave them all in the flitting, changing shadows of the stacks of woods or wherever it was that they were.

A sharp noise, like the cawing of a startled bird, came from somewhere above them.

George flinched. "Was that a crow?"

"Don't be ridiculous," said the Living Archive. "We're indoors. How could there possibly be crows flying around? Here we are."

She pointed ahead and the children saw a still pond, the water shining flatly without so much as a light ripple marring its surface. It had an iridescent sheen to it, as though it were coated in oil.

Tourmaline opened her mouth, closed it again, and finally said, "What…? How…?"

The Living Archive scratched her head and a small puff of dust escaped. "*I've* no idea where it came from, but then it's not my job to know that. All I know is that it's distinctly smaller than it used to be." She looked at Tourmaline pointedly and gestured to the pond. "Go on, then," she said, as if it was obvious what Tourmaline should do.

"I need to know where my mother is," said Tourmaline, in case the Living Archive had forgotten.

The Living Archive rolled her tiny eyes. "I'm an archive, not a psychic," she said. "We hold a vast amount of knowledge here but I'm neither a private detective nor a lost-and-found box. If you want to find that which is lost, consult the pool. I don't know *what* they're teaching up there in that university these days."

"Consult the pool?" Tourmaline looked at the Living Archive, then at the water, then at George, who was wishing he'd known that Living Archives were as prickly as they were turning out to be before he'd been instrumental in finding the way here.

The Living Archive just gestured in an impatient way then gave Tourmaline a surprisingly forceful poke with one of her bony fingers.

She approached the edge of the pond, which was still completely unmoving and cleared her throat.

"Show me where my mother is," she said, adding, "please", in case manners mattered to a pond. "Her name is Persephone Grey."

She waited.

The Living Archive sighed. "Foolish girl. Honestly. *Look into the pool.* What's the point of talking to it?

A pool can't answer you, can it?"

George stepped forwards hurriedly to stop Tourmaline doing anything that he'd regret, and together they looked down at the silvery surface of the water.

"What can you see?" asked Mai, who had joined them and so far could only see herself and Tourmaline flanking George, reflected back at her with remarkable clarity.

"Us," said George. "But maybe that's the answer? That we need to search within ourselves and if we trust in our own ability—"

At this point, the Living Archive scoffed loudly. "That's not the answer and I'll tell you that for nothing."

"Oh," said George.

Tourmaline leaned forwards and the toes of her shoes slid into the darkly rainbowed water. She inched back hurriedly, but not before her socks were thoroughly soaked.

"It isn't working," she said impatiently. "I can't see anything."

"Patience!" snapped the Living Archive. She peered at it herself. "Although, the water *has* been here a very

long time and it's not exactly at its best any more."
She glared at the children. "You'll be lucky to get
anything at all after everything it's done for us and with
you having been so difficult."

Tourmaline opened her mouth indignantly but
just then, a single large leaf floated gently down from
somewhere and settled itself on the pond, making the
tiniest little quiver in the surface tension of the water.
The leaf unfurled. It was green, and didn't look like it
had any business falling off a tree just yet.

A picture began to form on the surface of the leaf and
Tourmaline let out a startled noise.

Mai, who only saw a leaf, leaned back, caught
George's eye and frowned (the confused sort of frown,
not the concentrating sort or the angry sort). George
shrugged. Maybe this had all been a bit much for
Tourmaline. It was definitely a bit much for him.

"Ah, the old leaf illusion," said the Living Archive
sagely, as though she'd expected this all along. "We do
get more of that these days. Still very effective, if less
flashy than full-on teleportation."

"Tele—?" said George, forgetting his own

apprehension for a second.

Luckily, Tourmaline interrupted and saved him from having to fret about his own forwardness later.

"Why am I looking into the pond if what I need to see is on a leaf?" She was starting to lose the edge of awe she'd had since they entered the archives, and finding that her usual store of irritation was still there underneath it.

"Because," said the Archive, with a long-suffering air, "that's the way the trees here work. If they work at all. But you know best, of course. Do feel free to leave at any time."

Tourmaline suppressed a growl and turned back to the leaf. The picture on it was solidifying into what appeared to be a map.

George peered closely at the leaf. It really did look a lot like a leaf and nothing at all like anything else.

"Tourmaline," he said. "What are you looking at?"

"The map," said Tourmaline, as if that were obvious. "The … map on the leaf," she said, less certainly, as George continued to look at her blankly. "Can't you see it?"

George looked at Mai in case it was just him.

"I can't either," said Mai. "It's just a leaf, floating on the water."

Tourmaline turned to the Archive. "But it's right there, isn't it? Tell them."

"Tell them what?" asked the Archive. "That we can see something neither of them can?"

Tourmaline made several noises that indicated her general disbelief until George snapped her out of it with a quick pat on the back. "What does it mean?"

"Well, what do you think it means?" asked the Archive impatiently.

Tourmaline looked at George and George looked at the Archive cautiously. "That the map is only for Tourmaline?"

The Living Archive raised her eyebrows and opened her mouth in what was very clearly exaggerated mock-surprise. George's mouth became very small in response. There was no need, he thought, to belittle him. He was quite small enough already.

Tourmaline, meanwhile, was watching the leaf, which was perhaps listening to the Archive (she couldn't bring herself to think too much about how all this worked), because it drifted slowly to the edge of the pond where it butted gently but insistently against Tourmaline's shoe. She bent down to pick it up.

"Don't touch the water!" shouted the Archive. All three children jumped.

Tourmaline scrunched her toes inside her wet shoes. "Why not?"

"Well, go ahead and do it, then," said the Archive crossly, "as long as you don't mind paying for it." She produced something that looked like a well-used oven mitt from about her person, fished the leaf out of the water and spent an annoyingly long time drying it. Tourmaline used the time to quietly wipe the toes of her shoes on the backs of her legs and hope no one had noticed. Finally, the woman presented her with the leaf.

"I'm really the only one who can see this?" She looked at the map, which was etched into the leaf as vividly as if it had been the most brilliant ink on the finest parchment.

"Do you think it's where your mother is?" asked

George, looking first at Tourmaline, who didn't answer, and then at the Archive. "Is that what the map is for?"

"I shouldn't think it means anything else," said the Archive testily. "And it's the only answer you're getting because you only get one question with trees. They're absolute sticklers for it."

Tourmaline was frowning at the map. "It is," she said suddenly. "It is where my mother is. She said something about an island before she left, and I can see an island, right here. But who's going to use the map if only I can see it?"

"Well, *I* don't know, do I?" said the Archive, and walked off, muttering to herself. "Talk about ungrateful. You go out of your way to help someone and this is how they act. Become a Living Archive, they said. Greatest honour our family could ever know, they said. Bah. What, exactly…" Here she became inaudible and George, for one, was quite relieved.

"Can we go now?" he asked. "This place isn't … usual. Not usual at all."

They started walking back the way they had come and George gave up trying to catch more than a glimpse of the books on the way. No matter how interesting they probably were, they kept hiding themselves with moss and shadows every time he tried to look at them and he was beginning to think that they didn't deserve his interest after all. There were perfectly nice books in his bedroom that never hid from him and were always there when he needed them.

As the towering door came once again within sight, they passed an old man who was shuffling along reading from a book that seemed to be lit by an internal light that passed along the words as they were read.

Suddenly the man looked up, straight at Tourmaline, who sucked in a breath.

"Just you remember," said the old man, pointing a finger at her, "the source *can* change an artefact, but that doesn't mean it *should*." Then he added, "You know, the island won't let her go."

"Who?" asked Tourmaline, startled. "My mother? What does that mean?"

The Archive gave something between a rumble and a growl. "You'll find out, once it's too late."

Tourmaline looked at George, who shrugged helplessly.

"Excuse me, sir," said Mai, "but do you happen to know who Evelyn Coltsbody is?"

The old man frowned, his whole face lowering into an expression of suspicion.

"Someone who wants power," he said, "and it won't be good if they get it. Not good at all."

"Why not?" asked Tourmaline, her whole being concentrated on every word the old man said.

"Well, let it happen, then," he said, suddenly offended, but at what, Tourmaline had no idea. "See if I care. It'll only be a disaster. But nobody listens to us, do they? No, they think they can do a better job with whatever *they* decide is best. I don't know why anyone consults us. It's all nods and smiles when you give them the information they asked for. But do they use it properly? No. No, they just do whatever they wanted to do in the first place, that's what, and never mind truth or facts."

The old man stopped to draw breath and Tourmaline hastily said, "Thank you so much. We really must be going now."

She elbowed George and the children hurried

towards the door.

"I still can't believe that they're *people*," Mai breathed in the breathiest of whispers.

"What were you expecting?" asked the old man, lifting one tremendously shaggy white eyebrow with what looked like an effort. "Carnivorous books?"

Chapter Seven

Tourmaline had taken a detour to the kitchens on the way back from the Living Archives. There, she'd liberated a large quantity of baked goods while Mai and George kept lookout (cheerfully and anxiously respectively), and taken them back to her room, where all three children were now gathered on her bed.

Tourmaline selected a third sticky, gingery slice of cake spread with lemon icing. Persephone was still out there and in desperate need of rescue, but Tourmaline was a practical girl even when worried, and she couldn't find her mother if she was hungry.

"Is there anything better than a midnight feast?" she asked.

George consulted his watch. "It's not midnight."

"Close enough," said Tourmaline, who was more taken with the food than the exact time of eating it.

Mai licked her fingers. "I wonder if my mother knows about the Living Archives."

There was a short silence while they all wondered about their mothers and why they'd never been told that the Living Archives existed and how many other secrets their mothers had.

Then Tourmaline spoke. "If it's a secret only the adults know, they probably put it in the welcome pack when she got her job here."

George didn't think that was very likely, but he was still busy trying to come to terms with the fact that the Living Archive was what made his university the best in the country. There was a lot to think about. "Did you notice," he said, "how the first Living Archive didn't want to talk to you at all until you mentioned Evelyn Coltsbody?"

Tourmaline frowned, thinking back.

Mai leaned forwards and took two more biscuits. "No, it was when she said something about the source." She paused with a biscuit almost at her mouth.

"Or maybe George is right. But it was one or the other that made the Archive stop and turn round."

Tourmaline wondered if she hadn't eaten a few too many pastries. "But she didn't tell us anything about the source. Or about Evelyn Coltsbody."

George helped himself to another piece of cake. He didn't enjoy handling stolen goods, but cake was cake after all. "What are we going to do now?" he asked quietly.

Tourmaline decided she'd definitely had enough cake. The excitement of visiting the Archives was wearing off and she was realizing that she was the only person who knew where her mother was. There really was no one else looking for her, and *that* was something she didn't want to think about too much because of the panicky, lost feelings that came with it.

Some of this must have shown on her face because George said, "Don't worry. We'll think of something," and Mai said, "I don't think we should eat any more cake."

Just then, Tourmaline's bedroom door opened without warning, swinging wide as they all turned towards it.

"What, exactly, is going on in here?" Josie stood in the doorway, hands on hips. She took in the state of the bed, then narrowed her eyes at the large leaf sitting on Tourmaline's nightstand, then at Tourmaline's wet socks and shoes.

George tried to swallow the remains of his cake without chewing. Tourmaline surreptitiously brushed a healthy collection of crumbs from the bed on to the floor.

"It's my fault," said Mai.

Josie raised her eyebrows.

"I needed someone to talk to so I went to see George, and George, because he's very clever, thought that we should come to see Tourmaline. It's difficult being new but they've made me feel much better. I'm very sorry I kept them up so late."

George's heart was beating fast. Tourmaline waited to see what would happen. Mai looked contrite.

Josie's expression softened. Then her eyes narrowed. Then she seemed to have a brief internal conversation with herself.

"Well, you and George had better be getting back

to your rooms. All three of you need to go to bed. Maybe Mai could be comforted before lights out in future and preferably on a weekend rather than a school night. Is everyone hearing me?"

George had already bolted from the bed before Josie had finished speaking. He cast a glance of startled awe back at Mai as he left. Even Tourmaline, who was an accomplished liar when the situation called for it, might not have been able to think of something like that so quickly. Looking at Mai's innocent and artfully tragic expression, he wondered what else she might be capable of.

Mai cast her eyes down as she also left Tourmaline's room. "I'll see you tomorrow," she said and, after she passed Josie, turned and winked exaggeratedly at Tourmaline.

Tourmaline, who was used to being the one pulling off such daring stunts, found herself feeling a little put out, but she could hardly tell Josie what was really going on, and Mai had managed to lie in a way that actually made Tourmaline seem kind. It was altogether quite confusing.

"Tomorrow," she echoed. "Goodnight, Josie."

With an appraising look at Tourmaline, Josie closed the door. And Tourmaline, realizing she was absolutely exhausted, promptly fell asleep.

The next day, Tourmaline was in the refectory after classes before either of the others. She had caused a very minor explosion in her chemistry class that everyone had made far too much fuss about, then spent the afternoon writing an essay on why concentration and accuracy were important in the sciences. It had been a very trying day, especially as she was really only interested in getting back to George so she could talk about something that was actually important.

George hurried into the hall, quickly followed by Mai, who looked as though she had something significant to share with the others, which she did.

After a brief stop to collect a heaped plate of scrambled eggs for Mai and a sandwich for George, they both came to the table and Mai slapped a piece of paper down.

"What's that?" asked Tourmaline.

"A clue," said Mai. "From the lab. I put it in my pocket to show you but then the orchardist came and there was running and then we had to send George to see Professor Sharma and then we found the way to the—"

"Yes, all right," said George, who very rarely interrupted anyone but couldn't face the idea of reliving all the un-George-like things he'd done the previous day.

Tourmaline examined the piece of paper. "It's an advert," she said. "For a ship at the port in Brenia."

George, who was now curious, pulled it towards him. "*The Hunter*," he read. "Finest ship to sail the twelve seas. Commercial trips, cruises, and adventures to all destinations."

Tourmaline, meanwhile, had pulled the leaf from one of her pockets, where it had been carefully rolled, and placed it next to the advert.

"I brought this," said George. It was a piece of notepaper with his small and laborious handwriting on it – an exact copy of the note Tourmaline had found in Persephone's lab. It read, 'Consult the Living Archives??

Beware Evelyn Coltsbody!!!'

"All the clues," said Mai, tucking into her eggs.

"Also this," said George, pushing a piece of paper and a pencil towards Tourmaline.

"To draw the map," he said, "so we can see it too."

"Clever," said Mai. George smiled and Tourmaline promptly broke the tip of the pencil by pressing too hard.

By the time she had finished drawing, Mai's plate was empty and the refectory was starting to fill up with undergraduates.

Mai took the complete copy of the map, leaving a slight greasy fingerprint on it. "Are you sure this is right?" she asked dubiously.

"It's exactly accurate," said Tourmaline, looking from the beautifully rendered artwork on the leaf to her wonky drawing. It was the substance that mattered more than the style, she told herself.

"OK," said Mai, turning the map this way and that and then squinting at it. "Here's Escea," she said, pointing to a small country on the coast of a much larger continent.

"I know where we live," said Tourmaline, who had

actually been a little uncertain.

Mai looked at her out of the corner of her eye. "It's a good thing it's not a map of the whole world. That certainly narrows it down."

"Of course," said Tourmaline, who was relieved to see that now she knew it was a map of a particular area, she could work out where they were. She scanned the masses of land and the seas between, and her eyes caught on the island again. It was the only thing her mother had said to her about where she was going. An island. There was only one island on the map in front of her, so it had to be where Persephone had gone.

Tourmaline stabbed her finger down on the island. "She's right there."

"In the middle of the Skayqua Ocean?" asked Mai. "Are you sure?"

Tourmaline's eyes, and then her fingers, roved to the advertisement for *The Hunter*. She was a beautiful ship, with polished dark wood masts. The water sparkled under her bow and the blue sky framed her masses of bright, white sails.

George paused mid-chew. He had known Tourmaline

all his life, and he could guess the idea that was currently forming in her head. He hadn't thought that when they found out where Persephone was, Tourmaline would actually plan to go there. He really should, he thought to himself, have known better when it came to his best friend.

"You can give my mother the map now," he said. "That's what you're going to do, isn't it, Tourmaline?" He tried, and failed, to keep the faint desperation he was starting to feel out of his voice.

"I tried to talk to your mother, George. She doesn't believe that my mother needs rescuing at all, which is all Professor Aladeus's fault. You were right there and you heard it too."

"I know," he said, "but we have the map now."

Mai held up the blank leaf and then Tourmaline's copy, which even Tourmaline was prepared to concede wasn't very convincing.

George's chin retracted. "Well, yes, but—"

"Do you want to tell your mother how we got the map in the first place?" asked Tourmaline. "Or how I overheard Professor Aladeus saying no one is searching for my mother because I was in the space-between spying on him? Or how we made Professor Sharma—"

"Oh no. No, not – no." George pushed the remains of his sandwich away. "But there must be a way to make them listen without…" He tailed off helplessly. "And you can't just—"

"I have to," said Tourmaline. "You heard what the Archive said. The pond will only show *me* where my mother is, and the island she's on won't let her go, whatever that means."

"But how?" asked Mai. "You can't just buy a ticket and set sail to a random island. You're twelve years old and no one will let you."

Tourmaline opened her mouth to say she knew that perfectly well, which was why she didn't intend to ask anyone's permission, when her expression changed from annoyance to suspicion and then rapidly to understanding.

"Professor Aladeus is here and he's looking for me," she said.

George twisted round in his seat. "How do you

know he's looking for – oh."

The professor was hurrying through the refectory with a look of furious frustration on his face – a look that they recognized from many previous occasions when Professor Aladeus had found out something that Tourmaline had done or said or stolen.

At that same instant, George noticed his stepfather, Jacoby, entering the refectory. He had a stack of books under his arm, and when he saw George, his face brightened and he pointed to them with his free hand.

"It's time to go," said Tourmaline, hurriedly snatching up the coconut cake from the dessert portion of her tray.

Behind Jacoby, George saw his mother, the dean herself, moving past her unsuspecting husband and heading into the room.

"I think they might know what we've been up to," he said faintly.

He cast an apologetic look at Jacoby and a longing glance at the books under his arm.

Professor Aladeus, who was closest, had seen the map that Mai was still holding up. His angry expression suddenly changed to shocked, then delighted and greedy and triumphant all at once. Tourmaline couldn't be sure what this meant, only that it sent a lot of signals from her brain to her feet and they added up to *Run!*

She snatched the map from Mai and screwed it into a tight ball. "They know that *we* know that they lied about rescuing my mother." She locked eyes with George. "What if they're all in on it?"

"In on what?" asked George.

"Exactly," said Tourmaline. "We don't know." She looked at Professor Aladeus again. "How can we trust any of them? My mother's missing and I'm all she's got and they've come to stop me!"

For the second time in the space of two days, she found herself advising the people she was with to run.

Tourmaline sprinted for the window, surprised to see that George had got there first and had hopped out into the bushes. Mai darted towards Professor Aladeus, deciding that between him and the dean, she'd take her chances with the short professor. Josie appeared behind the dean and rushed through the refectory just as Tourmaline was swinging her legs over the windowsill.

"Tourmaline, come back here at once!" cried Josie.

"I found your wet shoes and I know where you've been, young lady. Don't you dare even think about—"

But Tourmaline didn't hear the rest. She only knew that though Josie loved her, she would definitely stop her from saving Persephone out of some mistaken belief that she was a child and therefore not capable of saving anyone. She dropped out of the window, fought her way out of the bush, and ran after George.

Chapter Eight

"George! The Stables!"

George cast a panicked glance over his shoulder then veered towards the Stables.

Tourmaline got a stitch and pressed her hand into her side as they ran. By the time they arrived, both of them were out of breath and shaky-legged.

"Where's Mai?" Tourmaline was already fumbling in the pocket where she'd stuffed the screwed-up map.

"I don't know," said George, looking around anxiously as Tourmaline pulled out her lock-pick kit. They were inside in a flash.

George looked down at the array of vehicles.

"What are we doing here?"

Tourmaline was still breathing hard.

"Where are we going?" He thought he already knew the answer based on the anxiety currently churning his stomach, and then Tourmaline confirmed it.

"Brenia port," she said finally. "If we can make it to the docks, we can find that ship."

George nodded, but Tourmaline paused. "Listen, George, if I get caught I'm going to get in a lot of trouble, and if I don't, this is going to be really dangerous. You're my best friend but it's not your mother who needs saving and you already went to the Living Archives with me even though you were scared—"

George opened his mouth to protest that he wasn't scared at all but Tourmaline grabbed his arm and carried on talking.

"What I'm saying is, I don't expect you to come with me and I wouldn't blame you if you didn't want to but I have to go now before they catch me, because if they do I'll never get another chance like this and I might never see my mother again. No one else knows where she is, and Professor Aladeus is lying about it and everyone believes him. I'm the only one who can save her."

George swallowed. "Of course I'm coming," he said stoutly, and his voice only shook a tiny bit.

"Oh, thank goodness." Tourmaline breathed out a long sigh and pulled George down the steps to the ground floor of the Stables, and the long, long aisle of vehicles.

George was worrying about whether or not he was wearing the right sort of shoes for such an undertaking when Tourmaline grabbed his arm again.

"Did you hear that?"

They looked up to the door. It was open.

"I'm sure I closed that," said Tourmaline.

"You didn't," said George. "But I did."

Tourmaline looked to her left, saw a motorcycle with a sidecar and made the sort of decision she was best at – snap. She bundled George into the sidecar and pulled a tight cap over her curls and an over-large pair of goggles on to her face.

"Do you know how to drive this?" George's panicked whisper made Tourmaline decide that she did. "And what about Mai?"

"We don't know where she is and there isn't time,"

said Tourmaline decisively. "As for this? It's exactly like a bicycle. Except that it's less work because you don't even have to pedal." And with that, she turned the key in the ignition. The bike lurched forwards, then shot along the length of the Stables, heading for the doors at the far end.

"Do you think we're going a bit too fast?" yelled George, who thought they were going a lot too fast.

"Not at all!" Tourmaline yelled back, even though she completely agreed.

But the motorcycle only seemed to go faster, and Tourmaline wasn't sure which of the handles was making it act that way. The door seemed to be speeding towards them, so Tourmaline closed her eyes and hoped for the best. When she opened them again, they were out of the Stables and on a road heading away from the university. The sun was just starting to set.

It took several minutes of zipping along the country lane, the last of the sunlight flitting through the trees that lined the avenue, before George could even begin to think about unclenching his fists from the front of the sidecar, and several more before his heart slowed down enough that he could speak.

"Do you know the way?" he shouted.

"Yes! I've been before, when…" Here, she tailed off and frowned.

"To wave Persephone off?" asked George.

"Yes!" She grinned at him, which made her look quite frog-like with the huge goggles on.

"Does it take long?" asked George, hoping hard that it didn't.

"It took at least half an hour when I went with Josie," she shouted. "But we're going much faster than that, I'm sure. I wouldn't be at all surprised if we were there in twenty minutes!"

George tried to muster a smile, found he couldn't, and nodded instead. The wind was whipping past his head and every part of his body was being bounced and jolted.

Seven minutes later (George was counting) he turned round to check behind them. There was something not quite right, even on top of the fact that he was rattling around in a sidecar being driven by a twelve-year-old who could barely reach the handlebars of the motorcycle.

At nine minutes, he turned again.

"What's wrong?" shouted Tourmaline.

"I think someone's following us."

Tourmaline swung round and had a good look.
"I can't see anything."

The motorcycle veered wildly to the left and
Tourmaline hurriedly turned her gaze back to the road
and righted it. After that, she clung on to the handlebars
and lowered her cap into the wind as she tore along the
country lanes, then the wider roads on the outskirts of
the town, and then the paved roads of the city. It was
terrifying and exciting and, as Tourmaline pulled up at
the dock, breathless and windswept, she wondered if
she'd ever enjoyed herself more. She tugged off the cap
and goggles. Her hair sprang back to its usual shape but
there was a faint line of goggle-shaped dirt on her face.

George slowly unclenched his fingers from the
sidecar, then got out very quickly lest Tourmaline decide
to drive anywhere else. His legs wobbled underneath
him and didn't seem to want to cooperate at all.

Tourmaline shoved the key into one of her pockets

and looked around. The streetlamps had already been lit, the water smelled brackish and looked murky, and the people walking around were not the sort she was used to, which is to say that none of them were professors or students. They were sailors and fishermen and dockworkers and, if she wasn't very much mistaken, some of them were drunk (she'd seen that before, though, since the professors did like their wine).

She took a deep breath as though the place didn't smell faintly of horse dung and strode off. George looked down at his shoes. They definitely weren't suitable. He ran after Tourmaline, casting a look back at the motorcycle, which was parked more or less straight, probably less if he was being honest. He caught up to her just as she stopped and stood there overlooking the dock.

There were colourful barges and simple fishing boats, one big liner that looked as though it would carry expensively dressed ladies off to the Adryan Isles, and a large, elegant ship that had acres and acres of white sail bunched up in rigging on masts that rose into the sky far higher than even the tallest tree Tourmaline had ever climbed. The decks were polished wood and the ship had a long, graceful prow with *The Hunter* painted in perfect cursive on the side.

Tourmaline pointed. "There it is! The actual ship from the advert. It's definitely a sign that we should use it to find my mother. You know, because she hunts … things?"

"It does look incredible," George said. "And very clean."

Tourmaline glanced down at her trousers. They were a little oil-stained from the motorcycle and the squashed remains of the coconut cake had made a greasy mark on one of her pockets.

George followed her gaze and then used his fingers to comb his hair, finding that it had reacted with as much shock to the motorcycle ride as the rest of him had.

A laugh – more of a cackle really – from behind them made them both spin round.

"She's a beauty, all right," said the owner of the cackle. She was the sort of woman that you might expect to own a cackle. She had grey hair, weathered skin, very blue eyes, and trousers that Tourmaline admired immediately since they had even more pockets than her own.

"Interested in that ship, are you?" asked the woman.

Tourmaline made her face look as though she didn't much care and shrugged. "I was just wondering."

"It's very beautiful," said George, and at that the woman smiled. She had a gold tooth.

"It is," she said, "and I hear it will be gone by tomorrow. Anyone who wants to board had best do it quick."

The woman joined them at the railings and they all looked out at the ship. It wasn't bobbing exactly, because bobbing was too small a word, but it was swaying with the current of the river.

"Where is it sailing to?" asked George.

The woman shrugged. "Here and there, somewhere and everywhere. There aren't many places that ship hasn't been. Almost anywhere you can think of is somewhere it's going to be sooner or later. I daresay it could take a person anywhere they wanted to go."

This wasn't a very specific answer but it did encompass the island that Tourmaline and George needed to get to, and they exchanged looks, each letting the other know that they thought it was good enough.

"Well," said the woman, "I must be away." And with that, she twirled round, her many-buttoned coat twirling with her, and left them.

George's stomach growled loudly and Tourmaline remembered the cake in her pocket. She pulled it out. It wasn't slice-shaped any more, but the crumbs still tasted good.

Tourmaline thought while she chewed, then said, "We're definitely boarding that ship. Right after we sell the motorcycle."

"Sell it?" It was one thing to borrow one of the university's vehicles, as long as they intended to give it back, but quite another to sell it.

"I'm still hungry, and how else are we going to get money for food?"

George couldn't deny the logic of that, so they ran back to the motorcycle … or to where the motorcycle had been.

"Where is it?" George looked around, as though it might be hiding somewhere. "Are we in the right place?"

Tourmaline pointed to the faint tyre mark on the road from where she'd brought the motorcycle to rather an abrupt halt.

"It's gone! Someone's stolen it! But how did they—" She felt in her pocket for the key, but that was gone too.

"That woman!" said George, looking outraged. "She was a pickpocket and a thief!"

Tourmaline shook her head in a wondering way. "You're right," she said, and the way she said it, George couldn't quite tell if she was outraged too, or admiring.

The truth was it was a little of both.

George looked plaintively at Tourmaline. "Now what are we going to do?" He was still really quite hungry himself and this was all beginning to seem the way things often did when he was hungry – much too difficult to deal with.

Tourmaline's face brightened. "I still have Professor Sharma's coin." She felt around in another of her pockets, then checked three more. "No, I don't have that either."

"How did she manage to steal that too?"

Tourmaline threw up her hands. "We're just going to

120

have to sneak on board and hope for the best."

She knew immediately she'd said the wrong thing. Tourmaline herself was quite happy to hope for the best, but George wasn't a hope-for-the-best type of person.

"There's bound to be all sorts of good food on board," she said quickly. "The people who travel on a ship that fine probably eat nothing but the very best, don't you think?" She threaded her arm through George's and hurried him back towards the ship, through streets that were now dark, lit only by intermittent puddles of yellow light from the gas lamps.

The water was black, sparkling where the light caught the odd ripple, and the docks themselves were shadowy.

"Where do you think all the crew are?" said Tourmaline, talking more to herself than to her friend. "And the passengers? Maybe they'll arrive early in the morning before the ship sails? But they'll all have tickets, I suppose, and we can't buy tickets because we don't have any money. They're not giving us any choice, George. We can't do anything but stow away and if anyone doesn't like it then it's their own fault."

George didn't fully follow this logic, but he knew that

Tourmaline's logic didn't always match up with his own, or anybody else's for that matter.

"Come on, then." Tourmaline marched towards the ship, which had a gangplank resting on the docks that went all the way on to the deck.

"What are you doing?" George glanced around, wide-eyed. "This isn't sneaking, it's just walking on to the ship!"

Tourmaline didn't break stride. "Well, how else do you suggest we do this bit? We have to walk right on like we're meant to be there. Josie says that if you do something with enough confidence it will look as though you're meant to be there."

"I don't think she meant that to be used in this context," said George, but by that time it was too late, and Tourmaline already had one foot on the gangplank and was testing her weight on it.

"It's fine," she declared, though her voice did wobble a bit. She stepped on, held her head up high, and marched on to the ship as though she'd paid for a first-class cabin. George scampered along behind her, trying not to look down, his heart beating uncomfortably fast, as it always did when he ended up doing something morally dubious with Tourmaline.

They stepped on to the deck, and something in the shadows back on the dock caught George's eye. "Did you see that? Something moved."

Tourmaline wasn't listening. "Where can we hide?"

George stared into the shadows for a few seconds longer, but all was still now. The back of his neck prickled and he shivered. But no one had challenged them, and the ship seemed deserted. For now. That wouldn't last if it was soon to set sail. Tourmaline was right – they needed to hide.

The deck swayed under their feet and suddenly George wasn't sure how hungry he was after all. "Maybe in one of the lifeboats?" There were two further down the deck, lashed to the sides of the ship.

Tourmaline frowned. She looked up to the sails, the rigging and the crow's nest, then back down.

George tried again. "Maybe we should get off the deck." He pointed to a set of steps in the middle of the deck that descended into the dark below. "The passenger cabins are probably down there. And maybe a kitchen," he added hopefully.

They listened carefully and, when all seemed quiet, went down the steps.

Tourmaline had been expecting corridors with neatly numbered doors, like a hotel. But what she was looking at was a small, roughly finished room, empty apart from four hammocks strung up between wooden posts.

"Where do all the passengers sleep?" Tourmaline looked confused.

There was a thump on the deck above their heads. Tourmaline and George exchanged a wide-eyed glance. The room they were in, which seemed to be crew quarters, was small – only a fraction of what must be down here inside such a large ship. She tugged George's sleeve and pointed at a door, just as there were several more thumps overhead. Boots hitting the deck, she thought.

George nodded frantically, and they ran through the door into a galley kitchen and through that into another room, only to be faced with several more doors. Tourmaline shot a questioning look at George, who shook his head. Tourmaline shrugged, opened the third door from the left since it looked the friendliest, and they stepped inside just as whoever owned the boots above thundered down the stairs they'd walked down themselves.

The room they were in had one small porthole, which looked out on the black river. It let in just enough light for them to see that the room was bursting with packing crates. Packing crates that looked curiously familiar. But Tourmaline didn't have time to think about it as she dived behind one and covered her mouth with her hand.

George followed her, crouching down and hugging his knees as hard as he could. The door opened and someone dragged something heavy into the room along with a lot of banging and swearing.

Then they went out and a key turned in a lock. Tourmaline and George looked at each other, then Tourmaline ran out and tried the door. It was locked, which she'd already known, but felt she had to try anyway.

When she turned round, George was digging through one of the packing boxes.

"What are you doing?" hissed Tourmaline.

George didn't answer. He tore through another box, flinging soft straw aside, then another, and another. There was a finely woven basket and he ripped the lid off that too, but all that was inside was an old rope, which he held up, frowned at, then dropped. Finally, when Tourmaline was really beginning to worry that George wasn't coping very well and that she might have to do something about it, he held up a small jade statue that looked somehow familiar to her.

George looked stricken. George often looked stricken, but right then he looked extra stricken.

"What is it?" she whispered, although she had a feeling she already knew. The packing crates and the straw looked familiar for a reason, and so did the statue. There was one just like it in the museum of artefacts at the university.

"I think I know why there are no passengers," he said.

Tourmaline's forehead crinkled. She waited for him to go on.

"We're not on a passenger ship," he said.

"No," said Tourmaline. "You saw the advert. It was…"

She looked around herself and then back at George. "What sort of ship is it, then?"

"The sort that belongs to rogue artefact hunters. And if they catch us we're probably going to die."

"*What?*" said Tourmaline, far too loudly. "We have to get out of here right now."

Just then there was a scuffling noise from the shadows on the other side of the room.

George's hand flew to his heart.

"It's a rat," whispered Tourmaline, which didn't make him feel much better.

But it wasn't a rat, unless rats could speak, because the shadow suddenly got bigger and a low voice said, "Stop right there!"

Chapter Nine

George clung to Tourmaline and this time Tourmaline clung right back. Her heart was beating wildly. They were caught, and the ship hadn't even left the docks. Why had she brought George into certain danger? Why had she thought that she could do this at all? Instead of rescuing Persephone, Tourmaline was going to need rescuing herself, but the only person who could come and rescue her was Josie, and Josie had no idea where she was.

The shadow advanced.

The shadow had two braids of black hair.

The shadow said, "I can't believe you left without me."

"Mai!"

Tourmaline let out all the breath in her lungs in one big burst. George put his hands on his knees as though he'd just run a mile or was about to pass out.

"What are you *doing* here?" asked Tourmaline.

"I'm part of this!" said Mai. "You left the university without waiting for me, so I followed."

"That was you following us?" George lifted his head, his hands still on his knees. He didn't trust himself to stand upright just yet.

"I took a personal gyrocopter from the Stables, and you're lucky I did. Everyone at the university is *livid*, from what I saw, and Josie was saying something about the Living Archives and Professor Aladeus said you wouldn't get very far because you didn't have any money or any food, so *here*, and you're *welcome*." Mai pulled a handful of coins out of her pocket and slammed them on top of a packing crate, followed by three squashed bread rolls. She stuffed one into her own mouth, glaring at George and Tourmaline as she chewed.

"Thank you," said George in a small voice. His fingers crept towards one of the rolls.

"Sorry," said Tourmaline, reaching for the other.

"We didn't ditch you on purpose, we just had to leave in a very immediate hurry. How did you get in here?"

Mai chewed hard, finding the roll more stubborn than she had thought. "I saw that you'd found the ship, and I was just about to come up to you, but then that woman arrived. She stole your keys, by the way. Did you know? Then you ran off somewhere but I heard everything you said to her and anyway it was obvious you were going to sneak on board. I didn't know whether to follow you or follow the woman, since she'd stolen your keys, but by that time I'd lost you both, so I came here to wait. Then you must have come aboard, only I couldn't be sure it was you, so I hid in here, and then you came in but now somebody else has come aboard and here we are." She stopped talking at last and swallowed the remains of the bread roll.

George blinked. "How did you happen to end up in the same room as us?"

Mai looked at him. "Because all the other doors are locked."

"So is this one now." Tourmaline's face had two worried lines on it right between her eyebrows.

"I wonder," said George, "why it was open in the first place." He looked around again at the packing crates, each one of them stuffed with a precious artefact. "What if we were thieves? You'd think they'd have locked all the doors on the whole ship if there wasn't anybody on board. And who was that I saw back on the docks if Mai was already on board? And what about that advert Mai found in Persephone's lab?" He frowned. There was something deeply suspicious about it all but he couldn't figure out what.

Mai picked up the jade statue from its bed of straw. "So we're trapped on a ship that belongs to artefact hunters. I thought you said Persephone Grey was the only real artefact hunter."

"I *said* that she was the most famous," said George, "not that she was the only one, but anyway you clearly weren't listening at all, because what I said was that *these* sorts of people are rogues and criminals, and—"

"Are we moving?" Tourmaline rushed to the tiny porthole. The lights on the far side of the river were definitely moving.

"We can't leave on this ship!" George turned round,

131

ran to the door, tried it again, then ran back to the porthole to see if he could open that. He couldn't. The girls exchanged a glance while they waited for George to accept the obvious – they absolutely were leaving on *The Hunter*, and there was nothing any of them could do about it.

George sat down on a packing crate and put his head in his hands. "I can't believe this is happening. Have you any idea how much trouble we're in? Have you any idea what these people are going to do to us when they find us?"

"Not really," said Mai.

George threw up his hands, which made Tourmaline raise her eyebrows. George wasn't someone who just threw up his hands on a regular basis.

"I don't think you understand," she said to Mai. "These people aren't like my mother. They don't work for a university. They work for themselves."

"They're ruthless mercenaries!" George put in. Tourmaline had rarely seen him so upset.

"They steal artefacts and sell them to the highest bidder," she explained to Mai. "They're the sort of people you find in black markets and if you cross them, they—"

"*That's* why the ship looks so perfect from the outside!" cried George.

Both girls looked at him.

"It's so they can sneak around and go anywhere they like and people like us stand on the docks and say 'what a beautiful ship'. No one would suspect they were thieves and murderers and—"

"Murderers?" Mai's eyes were wide.

"Well, I should think so," said George. "If you get in their way."

Mai looked around a little more nervously than before. "Do you think we're in their way?"

"Yes," said George darkly, and put his head back in his hands.

"We have to do something," said Mai.

Tourmaline stared out of the porthole, hoping that this would give her an idea. It didn't, but she did see the lights of the city clipping by at an alarming rate.

She watched as everything she'd ever known sped by, mainly because she didn't want to turn round in case

133

the small amount of panic that was now in her stomach made its way upwards. She didn't want the others to see that, and she didn't want to admit that she had no idea what to do next.

Persephone Grey, she was sure, never felt as though she didn't know what to do next. And probably her father, whoever he was, didn't either. He was possibly the captain of his own ship, sailing the seas, the wind in his hair, unaware that she even existed. It was likely, she thought, that he worked for the queen, carrying out secret missions that meant he could never reveal his true identity, not even to his own daughter, who he secretly wished he could visit even though the queen would never let him.

A few minutes later, Mai made a throat-clearing noise that was less about clearing her throat and more about trying to get someone to make a decision.

"It's very late," said Tourmaline suddenly. "It's totally dark outside and there's no way for us to get out of this room right now. I think we should try to sleep so that our brains work tomorrow and by then it will be light too and everything will feel better."

She wasn't sure she believed a word of what she'd just said, but she'd said it in the way that Josie might say the same thing (with authority) and saw some of the worry wash out of George's face as he nodded.

"Good idea," said Mai. She started pulling straw from the packing cases and made it into a sort of nest behind some crates. Tourmaline wondered if anyone else had ever said something with such certainty that the people around them did what they said, even though they themselves were trying not to let panic come out of their stomach at the time.

She and George copied Mai, patting and pushing the packing straw into something like a bed, and they all curled up in a ship called *The Hunter* that was taking them rapidly along the river and out towards the open sea.

As Tourmaline fidgeted on the straw in the dark she couldn't help but think about her own bed and the fact Josie would sometimes bring her a small snack at bedtime – a biscuit and some milk or an apple. She'd be quite glad to see the snack, and the person who brought it, right about now. Instead, there

was just an ominously creaking ship and no Josie.
Tourmaline curled up tighter.

Tourmaline woke up with a crick in her neck, slowly,
stickily, then all at once. There were people standing
above her. She pulled in a big, sudden, lungful of air
and scrambled backwards into George, who yelped.
Mai woke up, her eyes wide, straw stuck in her hair.

"Who are you?" Tourmaline's voice was high and very
young, and very much more afraid than it usually was.

All four of the people in front of them were armed
– one with many shiny knives that all looked as though
they could shave a solid oak tree into sawdust.

The rogue hunters advanced further, hemming the
children into the corner.

"I think the better question," said the tallest figure
looming over them, "is who are you, and what are you
doing on our ship?"

Chapter Ten

"It's her!" George hissed into Tourmaline's ear.

Tourmaline blinked and scrubbed a hand over her face. Her legs were aching and she felt as though she needed at least six more hours' sleep, not to mention a hearty breakfast. Mai scrabbled over the floor and pressed close to Tourmaline and George.

The rogue/criminal/possible murderer who had just spoken was the grey-haired woman from the docks. The woman who had pickpocketed Tourmaline and stolen her coin and keys, not to mention a whole motorcycle.

"You took my motorcycle and my coin!" said Tourmaline.

The hunter with the knives – a much younger woman

with light brown skin and blue hair – leaned forwards, her hand on the belt where the knives were sheathed.

"Your motorcycle?" she asked. "You can't be any older than eleven."

"I'll have you know I am twelve," said Tourmaline, absolutely outraged. "And that motorcycle belongs to the university!"

"So it doesn't belong to you at all," said the grey-haired pickpocket.

"Well… That's not the… You're a thief!" Tourmaline crossed her arms, both in defiance and to keep her heart inside her chest since it seemed to be trying to escape.

"And you're a stowaway," said the woman, reasonably enough, "and if I'm not very much mistaken, something of a thief too, Tourmaline Grey."

"I demand to speak to the captain," said Tourmaline. "I'm going to report this."

The woman laughed. "I *am* the captain," she said. "So go ahead and report whatever you like."

George had gripped Tourmaline's arm tightly when the captain had said her name, but she was too frightened and angry to realize it until the moment had slid past. Now she felt a bolt of the unpleasantness that you sometimes feel when someone knows more than you do.

"Wait a minute," she said. "How do you know my name?"

The captain smiled. It was almost friendly but there was a glint in her eye and her gold tooth shone. "You're a clever girl, you tell me," she said.

Tourmaline, who was used to having adjectives like "troublesome" and "infuriating" affixed to herself, but not so frequently "'clever", opened her mouth, then looked at George, who was shaking slightly.

"They know who your mother is," he said.

"Bingo!" said the captain. "Who doesn't know the great Persephone Grey? And who doesn't know that she's gone missing?"

That stopped Tourmaline's heart trying to escape because it nearly stopped it altogether. "Did you do something to my mother, because if you did—"

The captain's eyebrows went up and the blue-haired woman tapped her fingernails on her knives. Tourmaline shrank back.

"We don't know where your mother is. But we'd like to. She was on to something big." Here the captain broke off and smiled again. "Never mind that now. The important thing is that you're here. Perhaps you'll be more pleasant to deal with when you've spent a few hours locked in this room."

With that, she turned on her heel, and she and the crew left. The blue-haired woman closed and locked the door behind them with a smile as sharp as her knives.

Tourmaline swallowed.

Mai blew out a long breath. She didn't look annoyed with them both any more. She looked scared, and Tourmaline didn't blame her.

George was blinking rapidly – a sure sign that he was terrified.

They huddled together on the straw and sat in silence for several minutes before Tourmaline noticed George was looking at the jade statue again.

"You recognize this too, don't you?" he asked Tourmaline.

She nodded. "It's just like one from our museum."

George pressed his lips together. "What if it *is* the

one from the museum?"

Tourmaline looked at the door, then back at George. "You think they stole it?"

Mai got up, her face alight with ideas. "The captain did say that they knew your mother was gone. Maybe they came here to rob the museum of all the artefacts because they knew she wasn't here!"

Tourmaline's face prickled in a hot, unpleasant way. "If that's true, then were they the ones who ransacked my mother's lab?" The horrible sensation of it – of seeing her mother's most precious, private things tossed on the floor as though they meant nothing – came over her again. She scratched her head hard to get the feeling to go away.

George suddenly looked mortified. "Do you think they work for Evelyn Coltsbody?"

Tourmaline thought about it. "Maybe. But then why did she come back and search the lab again?"

George had latched on to his new theory. "Because *they* didn't find what she wanted, did they, so she had to go in and get it herself. And you," he pointed at Tourmaline, "had found that clue to the Living Archives that they couldn't find, and then Evelyn Coltsbody walked right in and took it." He finished breathlessly and sat back.

Mai opened her mouth to say something but just then the door opened again and they all froze. One of the crew – an older woman with brown skin, brown hair and a multitude of gold hoops in lines all the way up both ears – came back in with a basket covered in a cloth. She dumped it on the floor, gave Tourmaline a curious up-and-down look, then left, locking the door behind her.

Tourmaline darted over to the basket and ripped off the cloth. Inside were hunks of bread and large, smooth, green- and orange-skinned fruits. Tourmaline grabbed one and was just about to bite into it, her mouth watering, when George lunged forwards and knocked it from her hand.

"Tourmaline, stop! What if it's poisoned?" George was eyeing the food fearfully and longingly in equal measure.

"He's right," said Mai, looking down at the fruit. "Besides, we shouldn't really eat floor food."

"It's not floor food," said Tourmaline. "It's basket food, and besides, why on earth would they want to poison us? They could easily toss us over the side of the ship into the sea."

"Or use us as target practice for those knives," said Mai. "Or make us walk the plank and feed us to a shark."

"They're hunters, not pirates," said Tourmaline, but then she saw George's face.

"Anyway," she said quickly, "they definitely don't want us dead. The captain said that my mother was on to something big, whatever that means, and that it was important that I was here. And if they want us here, then there's no way she's going to feed us to sharks or any of that other stuff."

She retrieved the fruit from the floor, gave it a rub on her trousers (which were of dubious cleanliness but better than nothing), and bit into it.

"See? Perfectly fine," she said.

That was good enough for Mai, who took up a hunk of bread and tore into it. George, who was still worried, but also hungry, examined the basket. The smell of the bread proved too much, and there was no more conversation for several minutes until the basket was empty.

George picked at the crumbs in the bottom. "What do you think they want with us?"

"I don't know," said Tourmaline. "But they can't keep us locked in here forever. Where are we supposed to go to the toilet?"

Before George could express his concerns (he was sure to have some) Tourmaline crossed the room to the door and started hammering on it.

"Let us out! We all need a wee!" she shouted. "We'll have to use the packing cases as toilets if you don't!"

"Tourmaline!" George was scandalized both by the idea of using the bathroom in front of the girls and the thought that he could ever wee on a precious artefact. However, he couldn't deny that ever since Tourmaline had mentioned it, he really did need to go.

Tourmaline put her ear to the door and could have sworn that she heard muffled laughter, then the door opened, and one of the rogue hunters was there – a dark-brown-skinned woman with black eyes and tightly coiled hair.

"Captain Violet wants to see you," she said. "You can use the toilet first."

George didn't like the way she said "toilet", as though she was teasing them, and he liked it even less when he was handed a bucket and told to go up on deck and use it, then toss the contents over the side.

Mai caught Tourmaline's eye. They each knew the other one was thinking about escape. So did the hunter.

"If you'd like to try your luck, then be my guest," she said, as they walked back up the stairs and on to the deck.

Tourmaline ran to the side of the ship and looked out in astonishment. Then she ran to the other side, but the view there was the same – open ocean as far as the eye could see. It stretched out in every direction, blue-grey and green, crested with white, frothy waves and sparkling in the sun.

It was hot and the wind smelled of salt and newness and a wild tang she had never smelled back home. It was alarming and exhilarating and different and really quite as wonderful as it was daunting. She stared out at it all for several long seconds before the woman prodded her.

Captain Violet was up on the helm, steering with a great wooden wheel, the wind whipping her bright coat and her grey hair back. Tourmaline looked up. The great sails were unfurled, bleached white by the sun, and the blue-haired woman with the knives was up in the crow's nest, looking out to sea with a telescope.

The black-eyed woman nudged Tourmaline and shoved a pail at her.

When she'd finished and rinsed out the bucket with seawater, the woman was waiting. She shooed Tourmaline up the ladder to the helm and the other children away to the prow of the ship. George cast a worried look at Tourmaline and she tried to smile as she climbed up to the captain, but her face felt tight and she wasn't sure her mouth made the right shape.

"You wanted to see me?" said Tourmaline. She was used to be being asked to go and see an adult, but it was usually a professor, who was going to inform her that her latest English tutor despaired of ever getting her handwriting to look like handwriting, or that the cook was missing a large cherry pie and did Tourmaline know anything about it? She was not used to adults who were old enough to be her grandmother, wore coats she would have very much liked for herself, and were possibly about to throw her overboard in the middle of the ocean.

"It's time you told me about your mother," said Captain Violet.

"Who?"

The captain gave Tourmaline a look that Josie often used to give her – one that said "Don't try that on with me".

"I-I thought you already knew about her," said Tourmaline cautiously. It felt like she might be headed for some sort of trap.

"Tell me where she was hunting when she went missing. You must know."

Tourmaline thought of the leaf map, and the island, and how she desperately needed to get there. Then she thought about how her only way to get to the island was on a ship and that she was on one right now. Then she thought that she had no idea what Captain Violet might do if Tourmaline told her about the map.

She wished with all her heart that she knew what either of her missing parents would do, so that she would know what *she* should do.

"Why do you want to know that?" she asked, now thinking about what Captain Violet had said about her mother being "on to something".

"Tourmaline," said the captain, "you are not in a position to be asking questions. You are in precisely the right position to be answering them. Or at least I hope you are, because I would hate to put your friends in a position to be eaten by flesh-eating fish."

"Oh," said Tourmaline, thinking that the captain was a lot more fearsome than Josie, and that was saying something. "In that case, I'll need a map."

"I'm sincerely glad you feel that way," said Captain Violet. "Miracle! Bring me a map!" The black-eyed woman grinned, nodding at the captain and disappearing at speed down into the hold. She came back with a great scroll which she laid out on the deck before Tourmaline, weighting it in place with shining, transparent stones.

Tourmaline knelt down and tried to find the island,

but it was difficult. The map didn't look like the one she had seen on the leaf, and it definitely didn't look like the one that was still screwed up in her pocket. There seemed to be more on it, and things weren't in the places she thought they should be.

She frowned (sometimes that helped her to concentrate), but the island was slippery and refused to be found.

She pulled out the screwed-up map she had made but the time spent in her pocket had not been kind to it. It looked even less like a map than it had before and half the pencil marks had rubbed away.

"Tourmaline," said Captain Violet. "I don't know for a fact that the flesh-eating fish are hungry, but I've been at sea for a long time and I've never seen them *not* hungry."

Tourmaline looked at George and Mai. They were watching her, anxiously and hopefully.

Eventually she sighed because she didn't have any choice but to admit the truth (and it cost her to do so, because she did not want to admit that Mai knew something she didn't).

"It's definitely an island," she said, "and I definitely know where it is, it's just that Mai knows where it is even more definitely than I do."

"I see," said Captain Violet, raising one hand to a crew member who was now watching the other children. "Quintalle! Send the girl!"

Quintalle gave Mai a sharp poke on the shoulder and gestured to the helm.

Mai's ears turned pink but she climbed up towards Tourmaline, who moved over and tapped the space beside her in front of the map spread out on the deck.

"Show her where the island is," said Tourmaline.

Mai's eyebrows shot up. She searched Tourmaline's eyes. "Really?"

"I think it's best." Tourmaline didn't want to have to explain to George about the flesh-eating fish.

Mai bent over the map, her knees pressing into the polished wood of the deck.

She frowned. "It's not here."

"I think I've heard enough of this," said Captain Violet.

"What do you mean, it's not there?" cried Tourmaline.

"We *saw* it. At least *I* saw it, but I drew it for you!"

"I mean," said Mai, "that I know exactly where it was on *that* map, but it isn't on *this* map."

Tourmaline swallowed and looked up at Captain Violet, whose face had suddenly become unreadable.

"Show me," she said.

Mai pointed to a spot on the map. "It was there in the middle of the Skayqua Ocean."

"Are you sure, girl?"

Mai nodded. "It was right there, I swear it."

"About ship!" bellowed Captain Violet. She hauled on the wheel and the ship listed left in the water, the stones holding the map in place sliding across the deck along with Mai and Tourmaline, who tumbled into the railing. Laughter came from the crow's nest, and Tourmaline scowled at the sky as she righted herself.

"Where are we going?" she asked.

"Elsewhere, of course," said the captain.

She looked at Tourmaline in a way that made her feel as though she was still about to be offered to a hungry flesh-eating fish. Just one that wasn't in the sea. "But first, we need to make a little stop *some*where."

Chapter Eleven

"We can't trust Captain Violet," said George very quietly. "Did you see her face when Mai pointed out where the island was?" The three of them were looking over the side at the water churning by. The captain had dismissed the girls once she'd changed course and they had set sail for … well, Tourmaline didn't know where. She was slightly worried but Captain Violet had promised that they would go to the island and that was, she thought, really the best she could hope for in the circumstances.

"I saw her face," said Mai. "She wants something on that island. She already stole artefacts from the museum and destroyed the lab. I'm absolutely sure we can't trust her."

Tourmaline said nothing about the very recent threat of flesh-eating fish or about the way the captain had looked at her.

"We don't have to trust her," she said. "We just have to keep our wits about us and be careful while we're on this ship. As soon as we get to the island, we'll find a way to escape from Captain Violet, but until then all we need to do is stay quiet and out of trouble."

Tourmaline was perfectly right. So it was a great shame when the ship sailed into a horseshoe bay lit with a thousand lamps that evening, and she learned that they had no chance whatsoever of staying out of trouble.

The children looked at each other, before staring out at the lights in the bay while the captain yelled at the crew to haul the sails and drop the anchor.

Tourmaline didn't want to tear her eyes away from the enchanting sight of the bay. Its golden sand rose to rocks then to turreted buildings latched right on to the cliff side, pouring out their lamplight over the sea. Whatever else her trip on *The Hunter* was proving to be, it was exciting. The kind of exciting that she'd wished for when she'd looked at the photograph of

Persephone on her mirror at home.

She planted her foot on the bow and thought that surely her mother had done this very same thing and felt this very same way – as though she were about to embark on a great adventure. Tourmaline was sure that Persephone had told her all about it, though she couldn't specifically remember her mother saying that exactly. But it had almost definitely happened.

Captain Violet suddenly called everyone to gather on the deck. There was an energy about her that made Tourmaline think of Persephone when she was about to leave for a hunt. It made her chest ache and put tears in her eyes that she had to furiously blink away.

"Where are we?" she asked, to get rid of the feeling.

"I told you," said Captain Violet. "Somewhere. And we have work to do tonight."

The blue-haired woman grinned and tapped her fingernails on her knives. Quintalle let out a half-laugh, half-whoop that startled George.

"I suppose I'd better formally introduce you to my crew," the captain said to the children, "since you'll be coming with us tonight."

"What?" said George. "Why?"

The captain's gaze jumped to Tourmaline and then skittered away.

Tourmaline got an uncomfortable, suspicious feeling in her armpits and George frowned.

"The whole crew is going so I'm not leaving you here. You could very possibly steal *The Hunter*."

George and Tourmaline exchanged a glance. It wasn't that either of them thought Tourmaline wasn't perfectly capable of borrowing an entire ship, it was just that neither of them believed that this was the reason the captain was insisting they had to take part in whatever work the crew were doing tonight.

The captain ignored them both and pointed first at the woman with gold earrings who had bought them the basket of food. "Quintalle Nix. First mate, and the best chef ever to set foot on a sea vessel."

Second, at the blue-haired woman. "Dexta Decker. Weapons and munitions. In charge of keeping *The Hunter* spick and span and shipshape."

Third, at the black-eyed woman. "Miracle Jones. Languages, navigation, and top-notch sleight-of-hand skills. Now, go and eat something and be back on deck in thirty minutes because tonight, Tourmaline Grey, you're going to learn a thing or two."

The crew disappeared into the depths of the ship to places the children still hadn't seen and Tourmaline looked at George and Mai. "Why do you think we have to go with them?" she asked.

"I don't know," said George, "but let's eat something while we talk about it."

"I do think much better when I'm eating," Mai agreed, already heading for the galley.

They found perfectly cooked dough balls with buttery centres and some gingery biscuits that snapped when you bit into them then crumbled and melted in the mouth. There wasn't much talking or thinking until the food was mostly gone.

"I think," said George, "that the captain wants Tourmaline there for some reason." He had crumbs on his jacket and when he noticed, he picked them off and ate them.

"I think so too," said Tourmaline. "Also, I think Captain Violet knows more than she's letting on about my mother and I want to find out what."

"Last time you wanted to find out something from an adult who didn't want to tell it to you, we ended up on a stolen motorcycle," said George.

"Exactly," said Tourmaline. "And now we're on the way to the very island we wanted to get to." She said it as though she had planned every detail and it had all happened precisely according to that plan.

George looked at Mai and Mai shrugged. Neither of them could argue with that so they went back up on deck and stood looking at the flickering lights of Somewhere, which formed a glowing halo in the quiet dark of the evening.

"You're ready. Good."

All three of them spun round at the voice cutting through the velvet night.

A woman in a rippling, sequined evening gown, which slinked over her legs like shifting sand, walked down the stairs.

She had on pointy shoes and lipstick the colour of plum jam. Her hair was smooth and swept up on top of her head. She wouldn't have been out of place at the annual university gala.

Mai gasped, because the woman was Captain Violet.

"Oh!" said Tourmaline. "You look totally different!"

Captain Violet bowed gracefully, then straightened, winked and flashed her gold tooth, instantly ruining the effect.

Dexta glided on to the deck next in a glittering suit and false eyelashes that exactly matched the blue of her hair. Tourmaline spotted a flash of silver under her jacket and Dexta raised one navy eyebrow. She looked elegantly deadly.

Quintalle had some sort of uniform on – navy blue with polished gold buttons – and Miracle was wearing an orange-red lipstick that looked like fire against her brown skin. Her shoes had a hundred eyelets and were laced with a cream satin ribbon that twisted and crisscrossed up her legs.

Tourmaline looked down at her own clothes. Wonderful as her pocketed trousers were, they weren't going to win any awards for cleanliness.

Miracle looked at Captain Violet and some unspoken conversation passed between them. Then the captain shrugged and Miracle gave a small smile and shortly afterwards, Tourmaline was fitted with a pair of trousers with so many cunning folds and hidden pockets she had a hard time remembering that she was currently sort-of kidnapped, probably in danger and certainly about to be involved in something not entirely legal. She made sure the crew weren't watching, then emptied the contents of her old pockets into the new ones.

George, also in a new suit, was having no such trouble remembering that they were about to embark on something unknown and therefore worrisome as Quintalle lowered them all down into a rowboat that bobbed around on the silent, black water. She and Dexta then set to rowing them expertly across the sparkling bay.

Mai admired her gauzy dress, George gripped the side of the boat, and Tourmaline leaned forwards into the breeze as the lights came closer until they landed on the beach in the shadows and hauled the boat up on to the silky sand, cool gold in the moonlight.

"Excuse me, but might you be able to tell us what we're doing here now?" asked George.

The captain smiled and walked over the sand to a set of stairs carved into the rock, which led up and up and up until they opened out on to a wide stone pavilion.

The sound of violins and laughter floated out from doors flung open on to the pavilion, which smelled of summer and honeysuckle.

"We are going," said the captain, looking at George, "to steal an artefact."

George visibly paled. "Oh. I don't think I can… I mean, my mother would… I'd rather not do anything…"

"Think of it like this," said Captain Violet. "The necklace inside this building was once owned by a Pashviidan princess. It was made for her by the Frost King, so the story goes, and was passed down the royal family for generations until there was a great war. It fell into the hands of those who defeated the royal family and was lost for a hundred years until it surfaced again on one of the Midnight Islands in the hands of a wealthy art dealer.

"It was stolen from her a while later, then spent some time on display in a black-market gallery, but it mysteriously disappeared. It's been missing since before you were born, without the sniff of a clue until this past week when I heard from the friend of a colleague of an enemy that it had turned up on Somewhere in the private collection of the owner of this very house." Captain Violet swept her arm backwards to indicate the party that was going on beyond the curtains behind them. "Tell me, George, who do you think the necklace belongs to?"

George opened his mouth then closed it again a few times, looking like a startled fish.

"This is very often the way with artefacts," the captain explained. "Ownership is a much trickier concept than you might think. Take this for example." With a flick of her hand, she produced a coin from nowhere and offered it to Tourmaline. "For luck," she said with a wink. "Now come, we're on the hunt."

Tourmaline looked at the coin. It was her own, or the one she had stolen from Professor Sharma's study and Captain Violet had stolen from her. She wondered what her mother would think about what Captain Violet had just said. She wondered what *she* thought about it.

161

She didn't need to wonder what Josie would say about her having taken the coin in the first place, because that was very obviously something lengthy and not much fun to listen to.

The captain turned and swept the curtains aside, revealing an interior so plush and elegant, so richly adorned with velvet and damask, gold-fringed lamps and chests of polished wood, that George almost forgot what the crew were about to do.

"Why does she call it stealing if it isn't stealing?" Mai whispered to George as the four women swept into the party with the children following behind them.

George shook his head, partly because he didn't know, and partly because he too was trying to work out how he felt about it all.

Tourmaline had forged ahead, wiggling her way in between the crew to get to the captain, who was striding through the crowded room, greeting women in gold dresses draped on chaise longues, smoking cigarettes in long cigarette holders and wearing silk gloves that went up past their elbows.

Even at the university she'd never seen so many people wearing so many different colours and textures of material. There were women with feathers and sequins and shimmering make-up, men with shiny shoes and shiny hair, laughing and clinking sparkling glasses together. The whole effect was quite dizzying.

"Do you know all these people?" Tourmaline asked the captain. She had made her way up to the front of their party and was trying to keep her mind on what she wanted to find out, and not get distracted by all the interesting people and objects in the cliff-side mansion.

"Not a one," said Captain Violet cheerfully. "Darling!" she exclaimed to a woman with a diamond headdress. "You must come and see me soon!"

By now they had made their way through what seemed like several hundred guests, three large rooms, and a small art gallery of some sort. As they found themselves exiting into a large, marble-floored hallway with a sweeping staircase, the captain gestured to Dexta, Quintalle and Miracle, who all immediately splintered off in different directions.

There was evidently some plan in motion but

Tourmaline wasn't sure what it was. She looked down at her clothes. Obviously it was the kind of plan where Captain Violet had already known that there was going to be a party tonight and that they could all pose as guests.

"What did you mean by 'something big'?" Tourmaline asked quietly.

"What?" Captain Violet's gaze was flitting sharply around the room and she didn't look at Tourmaline.

"You said my mother was 'on to something big'. What sort of something?"

"The sort of something," said the captain, "that could change the world forever if it's true."

That didn't really answer Tourmaline's question, it just created a whole lot more and they all wanted to come spilling out of her mouth at the same time.

"But *what*?" she said, a little too loudly.

The captain put a hand on her shoulder. It didn't hurt but she could definitely feel it.

"What?" Tourmaline said, much more quietly.

"Your mother is a hunter," said the captain. "It's in her blood. Now, some artefacts are precious because they're old, because they tell us about our history, about where we came from and how we lived in ancient times. Some are fascinating because they tell a story of the way people's lives used to be. Some are just beautiful, the sort of objects that grip collectors in an obsession they can never return from.

"But some objects in this world? They might not be artefacts like the ones in your mother's museum, but they're artefacts nonetheless. Those artefacts are extra special, Tourmaline. They're downright magical."

Magical artefacts? The words sent a shiver down Tourmaline's spine. But did the captain really mean actual magic? Tourmaline gave herself a little shake to get rid of the shiver.

"Which sort is the one we came for tonight?"

"The second sort, I hope," said the captain. "Now come with me. And no more questions."

Tourmaline wanted to ask a *lot* more questions. Was Persephone hunting a magical artefact? But no, her mother wasn't hunting an artefact at all, magical or otherwise, so what was the captain talking about?

Maybe she was just trying to avoid telling Tourmaline

what the "something big" was. Tourmaline had some experience of evading questions in the classroom and she wondered if the captain's reason for not answering was the same as her own often was – that she didn't know.

Maybe it all had something to do with the mysterious source, or the mysterious Evelyn Coltsbody. Or both. Or possibly neither. Such a lot had been crammed into the past few days that it had all blurred a bit and she couldn't remember everything.

There were people gliding up and down the stairs as Captain Violet ascended followed by the children, so Tourmaline took the opportunity to glance back at Mai and George. George's head was swivelling this way and that at the paintings lining the curved wall of the staircase and Mai's mouth was open, her head tilted back to look up at the ceiling as she walked.

Tourmaline looked up too. The ceiling was covered in a myriad of mirrors, all cut and angled to somehow show every aspect of the person who was looking up at them. She could see herself in more detail than she had ever supposed was possible, from every coil of hair on her head and freckle on her face, to the thread in every last button on her borrowed clothes.

She reached the top step without realizing and tripped, ripping her gaze away from the ceiling and catching herself just before she fell face first on to what had now become a cherrywood floor.

"It should be right…" said Captain Violet, "… here!"

She abruptly turned left into a hallway and then left again into a room with a vast round bed covered in pillows that Tourmaline couldn't help comparing to her bed of packing straw aboard *The Hunter*.

"What are we doing in here?" asked Mai.

"This is where the necklace is, of course." Captain Violet glanced up and down the hallway, closed the door, and swiftly attacked a tall floor-standing vase. She took it in a bear hug and rolled it on its base to one side, revealing a safe in the floor that was the exact circumference of the vase itself.

"How did you know that was there?" asked Tourmaline, at the same time as Mai said, "Is the necklace in there?"

Captain Violet grinned, flashing her gold tooth.

George put his hands in his hair. "We can't just

walk in and take it!"

"Why not?" asked the captain.

"It – it just doesn't work like that!"

"I think you'll find that it really does, rather more often than you might think."

The captain put her ear close to the safe and started spinning the dial.

George couldn't believe that this was really how people hunted artefacts. He felt certain there should be more to prevent them from doing this sort of thing and he looked around in anguish. "Isn't there some sort of alarm?"

"That's what Miracle is for. She didn't get that name for nothing," said the captain.

"What if somebody comes in?" asked Mai.

"That's what Quintalle is for. Would you say no to her?" said the captain.

"But how are we going to get out of here with a stolen necklace?" asked Tourmaline, eyeing the necklace as the safe popped open and the captain pulled out a black velvet tray.

"That's what Dexta is for," said the captain, as a

grappling hook that looked like, and might well have been, a small anchor, hit the windowsill behind them.

"This can't be happening," said George, looking at the enormous emerald, shining like a rockpool on a sunny day and surrounded by several hundred diamonds sparkling as though they had their own internal source of light.

"And yet, it is," said the captain quite happily as she put the necklace on herself.

Just then, shoes clicked loudly in the hallway outside. The door flew open and Quintalle burst in, breathless and wide-eyed and obviously enjoying herself immensely.

"Out," she ordered. "Right now."

Chapter
Twelve

Without stopping to explain, Quintalle ran straight for the window and hopped on to the sill, pausing to admire the necklace round the captain's neck before disappearing into the night.

Several dozen loud voices sounded on the stairs, along with the clicking of high heels, as if the whole party was moving towards the bedroom where they all stood.

"Oh dear," said George. "Oh no."

Mai looked at Tourmaline and headed for the window, leaning out to see Dexta and Quintalle anchoring a sort of zipline between the window and the gardens below.

Captain Violet strode forwards, kicked off her shoes, pulled a small device from one of her pockets and swung herself out on to the sill.

She turned round to the children. "Are you coming?" She shoved something into Tourmaline's hands and then she slid down the zipline, disappearing into the dark.

Tourmaline looked at the devices in her hands. They were the same as the one the captain had used to slide down the wire – little curved pieces of tough material flanked by two handholds. Then she looked at George.

"It's up to you, Tourmaline," he said. "It's your mother we're rescuing."

"Whatever we're doing, we should do it very quickly." Mai glanced at the door. It was still closed but wouldn't be for long.

Tourmaline thought faster than she ever had before. She only had one main idea – that her mother was in danger and that it was awful having a mother in danger, and that she'd do anything to make it not true any more.

"We're going with Captain Violet," she said. "That's how we get to the island. Mai, you go first." She gave the other girl a pointed look, then a meaningful glance at George and handed her one of the devices. Mai nodded, understanding that Tourmaline meant to sandwich him between the pair of them.

"They really had this whole thing planned," she marvelled, and without a backwards glance, she dropped out of the window on to the zipline and sailed off into the night.

"You have to go next," said Tourmaline, pressing a device into George's hands and hustling him towards the window.

His body resisted the hustling, his back pressing into her hands. "I don't think I can."

Tourmaline had known George their whole lives and had therefore been thinking about how to deal with getting him out of the window ever since she realized they were going to have to use the zipline.

"George, if we don't do this right now a lot of very angry people are going to burst through the door and we are going to have to explain why we walked into this party and stole a priceless artefact right out from under their noses. It will be a very big and very long *confrontation*."

George visibly gulped and Tourmaline really did feel bad that she'd had to use the word "confrontation", one of George's least favourite. But it was for his own good, and as he nodded slightly, she tugged and pushed him on to the windowsill, telling herself that she would make it up to him later. And when she gave him a sharp shove and sent him screaming down the zipline, she added that to the list of things she had to make up for.

Her own ride down sent her stomach into her feet and back up into her chest. It didn't settle in the right place until she'd reached the ground where the others were waiting for her in a jasmine-scented garden.

Dexta flicked the wire, and the grappling hook or anchor or whatever it was unlatched from the windowsill and fell to the ground, where she gathered it up.

Faces appeared at the window Tourmaline had just exited. They did not look happy. "Aren't we on the wrong side of the house to get back to the ship?" she asked breathlessly.

"We are. But we're not going back to the ship," said Captain Violet.

Tourmaline looked at George, suddenly wondering if she'd made the right choice in sticking with the crew of *The Hunter*. "But my mother," she protested. "You said we were going to the island."

"And we are," said the captain. "Right after we drop this necklace off with its new owner."

With that, she strode off, completely barefoot, out of the garden and on to a tiny twisting street that led them deep into Somewhere. A few twists and turns away, they could hear sounds that sparked a hurried conversation between Captain Violet and Quintalle, in which the captain used the word "mob" and Quintalle (rather gleefully) used the word "angry".

The sounds seemed to be getting nearer. Tourmaline glanced at George to see how he was taking the evening's events so far. He had such a strange look on his face that she stared at him, even when the sounds of the crowd got louder and the captain advised that they should start running again.

"What will they do if they catch us?" Mai asked Miracle.

"They seem civilized," Miracle answered, "so I shouldn't think it would be any worse than life in prison."

Mai ran faster, as Tourmaline asked George, "Are you OK? You don't look quite right."

George smiled. "That made the Living Archives seem like they weren't scary at all," he said, in a marvelling sort of way. "It's funny, isn't it, how something so extra scary can happen that it makes you wonder why you were ever scared of the thing you were scared of before. If you see what I mean."

"George," said Captain Violet. "Could you maybe enjoy this epiphany a little later? When we aren't running for our lives?"

The streets were unlit and quiet beyond the lights in the bay. All Tourmaline could hear was her own loud breath and the Captain's next to her. Which was why she noticed when it suddenly stopped because Captain Violet disappeared. One second she was there, the next she was gone. Tourmaline stopped and George ran into her.

She spun round, backed up a few steps, and peered into what might have been a doorway, or just a deep shadow recessed into the stone wall that lined the street.

The crowd was getting close now – voices and echoing footsteps. Tourmaline could no longer tell where the sound was coming from, and since all the dark, twisting little streets looked the same, she had no idea where she was. Somewhere had begun to feel like a maze.

"In here!" hissed a voice, then the shadow she had been peering at receded slightly, a hand shot out of the dark, and she was hauled into a narrow passageway, followed closely by Mai, George, Dexta and Miracle. Quintalle pulled the door closed just as a stampede of polished shoes thundered past, the people wearing them all talking loudly. There was a loud *pop* that might have been a firework or a crossbow or a bottle of champagne being opened, and the noise moved on. Tourmaline breathed out.

"This way," said Captain Violet, who had grabbed Tourmaline from the street. They were crammed into a narrow, dimly lit hallway and she was already taking the lead, away from the street and towards strange music that came from somewhere deep inside the building, which abruptly opened up into a courtyard. The floor was laid with a mosaic of blue and silver and white tiles and there were ponytail palms growing everywhere she could see. The music was coming from a balcony above, which was strung about with glowing bulbs on strings. The lights seemed to give off a faint hum. There was a fountain in the middle of the courtyard, and when the children entered, the music stopped.

"Wait here," said Captain Violet.

She disappeared into the house, and when Tourmaline turned round, the rest of the crew had vanished too.

She frowned. "How do they do that?"

"I don't know, but I'd like to learn," said Mai.

Tourmaline suddenly had the sense that she was being watched. That strange, suspicious feeling that she'd had earlier returned. She looked up to the balcony. It was hard to see past the fuzzy yellow light emitting from the bulbs in the courtyard, but it was clear that the captain was up there and that she was talking to someone. It was a man, tall, with white skin and curly hair, Tourmaline thought, but she couldn't be sure. They were both looking down at her, and the captain was whispering furiously as the man stared intently.

"Who's that?" George asked quietly.

"I don't know," said Tourmaline.

"Then why is he staring at you?" asked Mai.

"I don't know," said Tourmaline. "But I feel like this might be why Captain Violet insisted on us coming here. I'm going to find out."

She walked forwards, meaning to follow the path the captain had taken, but she'd barely put her foot on the first step of the stairs that led up to balcony when the captain came hurrying down.

"Time to leave," she said. The beautiful (and very stolen) necklace she had been wearing was gone.

"Who is that up there?" asked Tourmaline, not moving from the step.

"I told you," said the captain. "The buyer of the artefact. Now he has the necklace and we need to leave. Or have you forgotten where we're going now?"

Tourmaline paused. "We're going to the island?"

"Absolutely. I told you we were going to Elsewhere just as soon as we'd been to Somewhere and I'm a woman of my word. Sometimes," said the captain, taking the opportunity to fold Tourmaline's arm round her own and tow her briskly back into the courtyard, much as Tourmaline herself often towed George. It was how Tourmaline knew that she was definitely being hurried along so she couldn't ask questions, and/or was possibly being lied to.

She stopped again and crossed her arms so the captain couldn't use them. "Do you promise that we're going straight to that island right now, without any more stops on the way?"

Captain Violet glanced up at the balcony over Tourmaline's shoulder, just for a second, but long enough for Tourmaline to notice and spin round. A shadow moved and then it was gone. No one was there.

"We can leave for the island immediately," said the captain. "Now let's make haste for the ship before someone realizes it belongs to us and does something tiresome like sinking it."

Tourmaline imagined Persephone's face when she, Tourmaline, strode fiercely on to the island and rescued her. Persephone would be tied up, perhaps in a cave, and Tourmaline would find her, put a finger to her lips, outwit the kidnapper, who was probably someone working for Evelyn Coltsbody, and triumphantly release her mother. "*Tourmaline!*" her mother would cry. "*How clever and brave and intrepid you are!*" and "*I would have been lost forever without you!*"

"Which way?" said Tourmaline.

Chapter Thirteen

Tourmaline awoke with a start in her bed of packing straw aboard *The Hunter*. She was still wearing the borrowed clothes, the jacket now a bit sandy and stained with salt water from their escape from Somewhere. There was little light coming in through the porthole but she could see the dark lumps that were George and Mai still sleeping. It was nowhere near dawn, but something had woken her – eyes staring down at her from a balcony, or at least a dream about them.

She got up, sneaking out of the room and heading to the deck via the galley (where she helped herself to several biscuits and a banana). The night was dark, the wind was fresh off the sea, and clouds chased restlessly across the sky trying to cover every star. Tourmaline's bare feet were silent as she came up the stairs to the deck.

"When?"

Tourmaline paused at the top of the stairs. The captain's voice carried down to her even though she was speaking quietly.

"Half a day, maybe a little more if the winds go in our favour." The other voice belonged to Dexta, and Tourmaline felt a slow smile creep across her face. They were really going to the island? And they were that close?

"Will they catch us before we get there?"

Tourmaline's smile dropped.

"Hard to say, captain. They could gain on us."

Captain Violet sighed loudly. "Could you see who it is? What flag do they fly?"

Tourmaline leaned out against the railings, pushing herself on to her tiptoes.

Dexta, when she answered, sounded grim. "I think it's the Agency, Captain."

Tourmaline strained her ears.

"Captain? I said it's the Agency for the Investigation

and Classification of Magical Artefacts."

"I heard you. I know who the AICMA are," snapped the captain.

Tourmaline recoiled. Her voice was so unusually harsh.

"Orders, Captain?" Dexta sounded cooler now.

"Full speed ahead, Decker. We must reach that island before the AICMA do."

"And after that?" asked Dexta.

Tourmaline waited, but the captain didn't answer.

She crept back to the hold, silently closing the door behind her and tiptoeing across the room. There was no way she was going to be able to sleep now.

"Where have you been?" Mai's voice was a whisper but it still made her jump.

She looked over at George, who was still asleep.

Mai sighed and pushed herself up to sit cross-legged. "Look, I know you and George have known each other forever but I'm here too, and I'm really quite clever. I could probably help if you'd stop scowling and tell me."

Tourmaline paused. She couldn't see Mai's face very

well but after a few seconds she saw the other girl's shoulders slump.

"I can't help the scowling," she said. "That's just my face." And she went over to sit next to Mai and told her what she'd just overheard.

"So there's someone chasing us in a ship?"

Tourmaline nodded.

"And it seems like it's the sort of someone who chases rogue artefact hunters?"

"I think so," said Tourmaline. "Captain Violet definitely didn't want them to catch us up."

Mai looked around them at the hoard of artefacts. "Well, it's pretty obvious why." She frowned. "But these things aren't magical. Are they?"

Tourmaline shook her head. "I don't think so." She didn't want to say it, but she was wondering if there really were magical artefacts, and if so, had her mother known? And if she had, why had she never told Tourmaline? If anyone would know about magical artefacts, it would be the most famous hunter in the world, and Tourmaline was her only daughter. It was embarrassing not to know and, even worse, it made her feel like she understood her mother even less.

"Anyway," she said, blinking in case her eyes were shining, "we don't want these people, whoever they are, catching up to us either. If they catch *The Hunter*, they'll stop us going to the island, and then I'll never find my mother."

George stirred, then sat up quickly. "What's going on?"

After they told him, George was quiet, his arms clasped round his knees. "Why are there so many things in the world that we just never knew about?"

"We can't be expected to know everything," said Mai. "We're twelve. Sometimes we don't even know things about people in our own families."

"What do you mean?" asked Tourmaline. It felt as though Mai was working her way around to saying something important.

But George's head had gone up, the way it did when something occurred to him. "Some people *do* know more than us, though. Do you remember what the Living Archive said just before we left?"

"He said a lot of things," said Tourmaline.

185

"Something about carnivorous books," said Mai.

"No, not that," said George. "The other thing. He said, 'the source *can* change an artefact but that doesn't mean it *should*'. What if the source is how magical artefacts become magical? What if it's literally the source of the magic?"

Tourmaline scrambled on to her knees. "Captain Violet said my mother was on to something big. And the dean said she wasn't hunting an artefact, she was hunting something else."

"I think," said George, "that we might find more than your mother on this island."

When the three children emerged on to the deck in the morning, Miracle was halfway up the rigging. She nodded to the captain, who was at the wheel. Tourmaline's eyes felt scratchy and sore. She'd stayed awake for a long time trying not to think about Persephone and how it felt to have had to work everything out for herself because her mother hadn't told her.

"Good news!" Captain Violet yelled down to them.

"We're making excellent time. Dexta should be able to spot the island soon."

Dexta was up in the crow's nest with a long spyglass and *The Hunter* was flying along, sails full mast, towards the early morning sun that was making the waves glisten. Tourmaline's heart swooped and she covered her excitement by running to the prow and scouring the horizon. Clouds hung low in the morning light, seeming to skim the sea itself. She had no idea how Dexta could see anything at all. Salt spray stung her face and she squinted until her eyes watered, but the island remained out of sight.

George touched her shoulder and tilted his head behind them. Tourmaline glanced at the captain to make sure she wasn't looking, then strolled back along the deck towards the stern.

Mai was already there. She pointed. There was the other ship, still following them – a small but determined shape on the water. It was a flying flag but at this distance and through the clouds all they could see was a patch of black and gold.

George planted his feet widely to help with the

tilt and roll of the waves as they watched the Agency ship. Tourmaline stared as though the force of her gaze could keep it from catching them and refused to move even when Quintalle served up breakfast. George, torn between loyalty and hunger, decided that he'd eat, but only because he could bring something back to Tourmaline afterwards.

Fifteen minutes later, he found his friend still there and pressed a hot, sticky bun filled with currants into her hand. She ate it in three bites, wiped her hands on her jacket and pointed back to the ship following them. "It's closer."

George nodded, then swallowed. He did that when he had to tell Tourmaline something she wasn't going to like hearing.

She frowned. "What is it?"

"I think you'd better go and see the captain," he said.

"Good," said Tourmaline. "There's something I want to ask her."

When Tourmaline entered the captain's cabin, she was poring over several charts and maps that were spread over her desk.

She looked up at Tourmaline. "Mai says that she's sure about the location of the island. Are *you* sure?"

Tourmaline nodded.

The captain frowned.

"There's – there's a ship following us," Tourmaline said. "Who are they?"

The captain narrowed her eyes but Tourmaline held her chin up, even if it wobbled a little. She was tired of adults trying to keep things from her.

There was a long and uncomfortable pause. The captain sat back in her chair and looked at Tourmaline in such a way that she could tell the woman was deciding whether to tell her the truth or not.

"They are the Agency for the Investigation and Classification of Magical Artefacts." The captain clasped her hands in front of her on the desk. "They're a group that follow up on any leads they have on artefacts that might be … out of the ordinary. Like the ones I told you about. And they are following us because I have a ship full of stolen artefacts."

Tourmaline blinked. "Are there magical artefacts on

board? Or just the boring kind?"

The Captain barked a laugh. "They're both valuable, you know. Just in different ways. The AICMA are only concerned with the magical kind, but in any case, they don't know *what* I've got on board, and I'd like it to stay that way."

Tourmaline bit her lip.

"Something else to ask me?" The captain returned her attention to the charts laid out on the desk.

"Who was that man yesterday? The one you're working for. Why was he staring at me?"

"I only work for that man when it suits me," said the captain. "Right now it happens to suit me because I'm considering going into business with him. Either that or double-crossing him, I haven't decided yet. But you don't need to concern yourself about that. He's only interested in magical artefacts and where they come from."

"You mean the source?"

The captain paused. Only for a second but Tourmaline saw it and it made her heart pound. George had been right. The source made magical artefacts.

She waited, but the captain didn't answer. She wasn't

going to tell Tourmaline anything about the source. Maybe she'd tell her something else, though.

Tourmaline breathed out. "Did you steal the artefacts from the museum at the university?"

The captain stopped using the little tool that she was walking across the chart and quietly laid it on the paper.

Tourmaline's heart kicked her chest. Maybe she shouldn't have asked so many questions. Maybe she should just leave.

"Yes," said the captain.

Tourmaline breathed in and out three times.

"Although," said the captain, "the jade statue didn't belong to the museum."

"Of course it did! It was right there in the museum and you took it out of the museum and now it's right here on the ship so you must have stolen it!"

Captain Violet shrugged and picked up the little tool from her chart. "I didn't say I didn't steal it. I absolutely did steal it. But it's been stolen before and it will no doubt be stolen again and the person who stole it right before me was Persephone Grey."

Tourmaline's outrage started in her toes and burst

upwards through her stomach and out of her mouth. "My mother is not a thief!"

Captain Violet looked steadily at Tourmaline. She was quiet for several moments – so long that Tourmaline calmed down enough to wonder what was going to happen next.

"There's a whole world out there."

"I know that," said Tourmaline.

"Places that you can't even imagine, and people in them who believe different things about artefacts, and about magic itself."

"I know that too," said Tourmaline. "Wait. What kind of places?"

"Places that aren't Pellavere University," said the captain. "People who aren't the AICMA. In fact, there's a black market in Escea itself that—"

Tourmaline took a little step forwards. "That what?" she said encouragingly.

"Do you think," the captain replied, "that it's fair that all the precious things in this world belong to people rich enough to go to a university?"

Tourmaline couldn't help but feel defensive about the

university. It was the only home she had ever known. "Don't *you* just go around stealing things for rich people?" she retorted.

The captain tilted her head and gave a little shrug. "Sometimes I do, and sometimes I don't," she said. "Sometimes I need to put food on the table and keep the ship shipshape and sometimes—"

"So you're a bad person," said Tourmaline impatiently. She knew it wasn't the kind of thing she should say to an adult, but she said it anyway. Captain Violet's answer still surprised her.

"I'm bad and I'm good. A little of both," said the captain. "Like anyone else in this world."

Tourmaline opened her mouth to say that that couldn't possibly be true, then closed it again because by now she wasn't sure. "Was it you who searched my mother's lab?"

"It was," said the captain. "But if you think about it, us leaving that advert for *The Hunter* worked out very well for you in the end."

Tourmaline's mouth fell open. "You left it there on purpose? So you *tricked* us into coming on board?"

"I encouraged you," said the captain. "But really it was more of a group effort."

"What does that mean?" asked Tourmaline, absolutely outraged.

Her outrage didn't seem to bother the captain at all. "You're on your way to save Persephone Grey, aren't you? Isn't that what you wanted?"

Tourmaline had no idea how to formulate a response to this infuriating logic, but she was about to give it a good go when she was interrupted by Quintalle bellowing "Captain!" from up on the deck.

Captain Violet looked at Tourmaline and they both ran.

Once on the deck, Tourmaline spun round in a circle. "What is it?"

In front of them, the endless undulating waves of the ocean disappeared into the mist.

Quintalle scowled a scowl that rivalled one of Tourmaline's. "I'll tell you what it's not. It's not an island, you foolish girl."

"But I saw the map!" said Mai. "I swear it was here!"

Captain Violet held out her arms, indicating the vast

ocean spreading around them.

George ran and looked over the port side down into the sea, then ran back across the ship to the starboard. He looked sheepishly at the others. "Islands do sink. Sometimes," he said.

"Is that what you expect us to believe?" asked Quintalle. "That this island you've led us on a wild goose chase to has sunk?"

"You practically kidnapped us!" Tourmaline said indignantly.

"You stowed away," the captain said reasonably.

"Elsewhere doesn't exist," growled Quintalle. "It never did."

"It has to be here!" Tourmaline joined George and peered down into the water. It was greyish, greenish, bluish, blackish and it was altogether impossible to see anything, much less an island. She had no idea what to do now. Her entire plan had hinged on getting to the island and if it wasn't here then she had nothing. Her chest felt as though her jacket was three sizes too small.

"It has to be here. But … it *isn't* here," she said.

Dexta jumped on to the deck. She had climbed down from the crow's nest and her blue hair was windswept, the tip of her nose red.

"Something else is, though."

She turned to the stern of the ship. Tourmaline gasped (something she wasn't prone to doing) and George looked at her before he looked past the mast and the sails and the cabin rising up from the deck. Then he understood.

The ship that had been following them, with its black-and-gold flag flying, had caught up, and was right behind them.

Chapter Fourteen

George stared at the other ship in alarm. "What are they going to do to us?" His voice was tight with panic.

Dexta took out her spyglass and trained it on the ship behind *The Hunter*.

No one answered George.

"The island has to be here!" said Tourmaline.

"Then where is it?" Mai demanded.

"This is why it's called Elsewhere," said Quintalle, glowering at the children.

Tourmaline flung her hands up. She couldn't have come this far and be right here where her mother should be only to get snatched away by the Agency.

She ran to the side of *The Hunter* and looked out over the sea again, desperately hoping that the island would show itself. The sun shone on the sparkling waves, blinding her, making her eyes water, and she looked down into the depths, where fish and whales and jellyfish lived.

Afterwards she couldn't be sure what made her do it. Maybe because she wanted the island to be there so badly. Maybe because she really was as contrary as Professor Aladeus said she was. Maybe it was just a bird flying by in search of a meal or migrating to some far-off land. But she looked up. The clouds parted a little, thinning into wisps and strands as though she was somehow making them dissipate by looking at them.

And there it was.

The island.

It cast no shadow, which was the least of the laws of physics that it was breaking, but explained to Tourmaline why she hadn't noticed it before. She closed her eyes for a very brief second and inside her head said to her mother, "I'm coming. I'm right here," so that Persephone would know that she was going to be rescued, she just had to hold on.

Captain Violet was holding a terse, unsatisfactory

conversation with the crew about what they should do, and Tourmaline had to shout "Stop!" several times before they stopped and stared at her.

"Elsewhere." She pointed upwards and they looked. The last of the clouds fell apart and vanished and they all stared. At the island. Which was motionless in the air directly above them – a great round clod of earth as big as, well, as big as an island, shot through with tree roots and looking like an enormous version of a potted plant upended and hanging in mid-air.

"Bless every artefact I ever stole," said Quintalle. "It *does* exist."

Captain Violet let out a string of colourful words, some of which George had not even heard before, but all of which he understood to mean that this was a very surprising thing. Dexta scrambled up to the crow's nest and pulled out her spyglass, peering up to scrutinize the island as though she couldn't believe that it was real.

Quintalle ran across the deck, possibly to fetch something, possibly because she didn't know what else to do. The children couldn't tell because none of them had taken their eyes off the island. It was the strangest thing that Tourmaline had ever seen, and she could tell from the way George was muttering about gravity that he thought so too.

She glanced at Mai and was glad to see that she too was so shocked her head was tilted all the way back and her mouth was hanging open. Even Captain Violet was stock still, staring, although she had a wicked grin on her face.

"Prepare to be boarded!" The cry from the Agency ship snapped everyone out of their trance. Quintalle froze, and everyone else looked at Tourmaline.

"I have to get up there," Tourmaline said.

George gave a small cough.

"I mean, *we* have to get up there," she said.

"How?" asked Mai.

Tourmaline didn't know, but she saw the look that passed between Quintalle and Captain Violet.

"What?" she asked. "What is it? We're about to be boarded and my mother is up there and if you know how to get to that island then tell me *right now*."

She stopped talking and swallowed. George's eyes couldn't have got any wider as he stared at the captain to see how she was going to react.

"Captain," said Miracle. "I think it's time."

"But in front of the Agency?" said the captain.

Miracle's black eyes were grave. "I think," she said, "that ship has sailed, so to speak."

"What are you talking about?" Tourmaline crossed her arms. Her heart was beating very fast again.

Captain Violet nodded at Quintalle, who scarpered into the hold.

"We have an artefact that might be able to help," she said. "The kind of artefact that the Agency would be interested in. The kind of artefact that we don't particularly want them to know we have on board." Here, Miracle cleared her throat loudly. The captain sighed. "But that we are nevertheless going to have to use in front of them if we mean to get on to the island."

"We *do* mean to get on to the island," said Tourmaline. She eyed the Agency ship, which was sliding closer, watching as sailors readied a long plank that they meant to use to board *The Hunter*. A silver dagger flew through the air and one of the sailors yelped and drew her fingers back. Tourmaline looked up to see Dexta, smiling a rather malicious smile and holding another of her daggers, tossing it end over end and catching it, clearly ready to throw.

It was magnificent, if terrifying, and Tourmaline made a mental note to ask Dexta to teach her to throw knives if they didn't all die in the next few minutes.

Quintalle appeared on deck dragging something Tourmaline recognized from the hold. It was the finely woven basket that George had looked into just before he'd found the jade statue from the university museum. Quintalle placed it in the middle of the deck and pulled off the lid with a flourish. Tourmaline peered inside, but all that did was confirm what she already knew – that the basket contained some old and rather frayed-looking rope.

"What's the point of that?" she cried, looking up again at the island looming above them, huge and real and *right there*, but decidedly out of reach. It was infuriating.

But as she looked to George and Mai in desperation, the strangest thing happened. The rope began to move. First it twitched, right at the end, and then it began to rise slowly, uncoiling like a snake sniffing the air. It rose out of the basket and kept going, shooting up into the sky until it reached the mass of land hanging above them.

"Well?" said Captain Violet. "What are you waiting for?"

"You can't expect us to—" George's protest was cut off by a loud bang. The sailors from the other ship had got the plank in place and, despite Dexta's daggers, one of the women had hopped up on to the plank.

Mai started towards the rope but there was no way Tourmaline was going to allow her to go first. She darted forwards, ignored George pressing both hands to his mouth, and began to shin up the rope, which felt exactly as filthy and rotten as it looked.

But it held her weight and she climbed quickly, not glancing down when she felt the rope moving as the others piled on below her. There was a great commotion on the deck of *The Hunter* as the Agency sailors boarded – Quintalle snarling, Dexta flinging knives that whistled through the air, cries and thumps from the other crew, Miracle shouting to Tourmaline to keep climbing and Captain Violet roaring furious curses. Tourmaline's hands cramped and her arms burned, but she thought

of Persephone and what she would do. She also thought
of her unknown father who was undoubtedly brave and
strong and would likely make short work of climbing
a rope, especially a magical one, and she hauled herself
up and up, her jaw set in determination, until she came
level with the island.

She could smell it – an earthy, damp smell of soil,
and something else, like a storm in the air, a hint and
crackle that lifted the hair on her arms even though she
was sweating by now.

"Hurry up!"

Someone shoved Tourmaline's feet as she paused,
clinging to the rope, her arms shaking. She looked
down (which is always a terrible mistake, but one that
every single person who has ever climbed something has
made). The deck was stomach-churningly far below and
suddenly looked much harder than it ever had before.
The rope still stood magnificently and impossibly in
the air, and just below her, Mai's light brown face was
flushed red.

"Move!" Mai said.

Tourmaline hauled herself up until she reached the

flat edge of the island, rolled on to it and immediately fell into another sea. She came up spitting salt water. Behind her the edge of the island stopped, and the sea with it, as though she were in a giant fish tank, the sides of which she couldn't see. The sky was blue, the sun was burning down on her head and some hundred yards in front of her was a thin fringe of beach. Beyond it, jungle rose thickly from the golden sand.

There was a splash behind her and Mai gasped and spluttered her way to the surface, her black hair plastered to her head.

"Swim!" she cried.

Tourmaline had enough energy left for a frown. This was *her* rescue operation and she didn't need Mai telling her what to do. She struck out for the island, her sopping clothes trying to suck her down, until her feet reached the sandy bottom and she staggered, dripping and coughing, on to the shore.

Mai was close behind, followed by Dexta, Captain Violet, Quintalle, and Miracle, who appeared to be dragging some kind of bundle as she swam.

Tourmaline scanned the water. "Where's George?"

"That," said Mai, pointing at the bundle Miracle was dragging, "is George."

Tourmaline flopped back on the sand in relief. Her arms felt distinctly noodle-ish and her eyes stung with salt.

Dexta was the next to reach land, her blue hair, which usually defied gravity, straggling limply on her collar. The rest of the crew followed.

Captain Violet strode out of the sea, water streaming from her jacket and boots, her chest heaving. "Best if we depart quickly," she said.

"What?" Tourmaline felt as though she could easily lie down and sleep but when Captain Violet pointed, she sat up straight. Someone from the Agency ship was emerging from the sea – a black-haired woman wearing glasses and some kind of business suit.

"She followed us?" Tourmaline looked up at Captain Violet, who shrugged.

"No way to stop her. There might be a way to control the rope, but no one has any idea what it is."

With that, she hastily carried on up the beach towards the jungle that fringed the sand. "Are you coming?"

Miracle had hauled George on to land, her skin glistening with water droplets. He was puffing hard and trying to wrestle his wet clothes back into some semblance of order.

Mai squeezed the water out of her hair, Tourmaline took George's hand, and the three children turned and ran for the jungle. The crew had already vanished into the dense foliage. The children were at the line of trees when a voice rang out across the water.

"Mai!"

Mai froze.

Tourmaline spun round. It was the same voice she had heard in her mother's lab, when she and Mai were hiding. The same voice that belonged to the woman who had dropped the handkerchief with the initials *E.C.* on it. It was Evelyn Coltsbody.

The woman with the glasses and business suit was still swimming, but she called out again. "Mai Cravenswood!"

"Who is that?" asked George.

Mai threw a wide-eyed, extremely shocked glance over her shoulder, then grabbed his hand and ran, tugging Tourmaline along with him.

Chapter Fifteen

As they ran into the jungle, George glanced at Tourmaline. She was scowling suspiciously at Mai. He had questions himself – a lot of them – but there was no time to stop now.

The jungle was thick and vividly green, and instantly Tourmaline felt as though a hot, wet blanket had been dropped on her from above. She dropped George's hand to fight her way through twined vines and shiny leaves, pushed in front of Mai, and led them away from the light and deep into the jungle.

"Tourmaline!"

George was out of breath. They'd been hacking and tearing, shoving and pushing their way through the foliage for several minutes.

Tourmaline paused. "What?"

George pointed. Tied to a tree were two signs written on curved pieces of rotten wood that looked like the hull of a ship. They were strapped to the tree with blackened, moss-covered rope. The first read TURN and the second, BACK. The letters dripped down the wooden signs, sticky and dark.

"Is the writing ... tar?" asked George. Tourmaline heard the note of worry in his voice. It was mixed with hope that what he was thinking wasn't true.

"It's not tar," said Mai in a whisper. "It's blood."

Tourmaline turned round to glare at Mai. George looked terrified, and Tourmaline couldn't help but think of *The Hunter*'s smooth, curved hull, torn to pieces along with her crew, and maybe her passengers too.

"We should go back," said George, and it was the first time since they'd left the university that he'd sounded truly certain. "Tourmaline, this isn't a game."

"I know it's not," she said. "It's me rescuing..."

"Persephone?" said George, frowning.

"Exactly," said Tourmaline. "It's my mother. So I can't go back. I have to go on."

She turned to Mai and crossed her arms. "But first I want to know how that woman from the Agency for the Investigation and Classification of Magical Artefacts knew your name. Who are you?"

Mai wrapped her own arms around her body. "You know who I am. I'm Mai."

"Mai Cravenswood," said Tourmaline. "Just like that lady called out when she was chasing us." She took a step forwards. "I remember her voice, Mai. She's the woman from the lab. She's Evelyn Coltsbody and you know it, so tell us the truth!"

Mai shook her head. "You're wrong."

Tourmaline took another step forwards. "You're lying! I was right there. It's the same woman."

"I'm not a liar! That's not what I meant!" Mai's arms were unfolded now and she threw them up in the air. "That woman is *not* Evelyn Coltsbody."

George, who had been hovering between them really hoping that they would stop arguing, said, "Maybe we should get out of here first and discuss this later?"

Tourmaline didn't usually ignore George but right then she barely heard him. "Who is she, then?"

"Her name," shouted Mai, "is Emiko Cravenswood and I know because she is my *mother*!"

Tourmaline's breath came out in a big whoosh.

"Tourmaline," said George.

"You're a spy!" Tourmaline didn't even look at George. He took hold of her arm and tugged.

"Tourmaline!"

Tourmaline finally swung round to glare at George. "What?"

"Look!" George pointed down. There were a few insects crawling on the soft, peaty earth.

"George," said Tourmaline crossly. "We're in a jungle. There are bound to be some bugs."

"I understand that," said George, his pointing finger trailing back to direct her gaze down the path they'd just made. "But what if there are more than 'some'?"

The ground was alive – a crawling mass of insects, flowing through and over the vines and plants like a wave. A very fast-moving wave that was coming straight for them.

"Oh," said Tourmaline.

"Can we run now?" asked George.

"Yes," said Tourmaline. "I think that would be a good idea."

She turned tail and ran, blindly pushing through the jungle, straight past the sign that said TURN BACK, and George followed right behind her. Tourmaline tripped, George's legs got badly scratched, something bit Tourmaline on the back of her neck, and still they ran.

A few minutes later, totally out of breath, very sweaty, and completely exhausted, they came to a stop in a darkly shaded dip in the jungle. Tourmaline scratched her bite, George pressed his fingers into the stitch in his side, and they both waited a few seconds, staring around, panting for breath in the thick, hot air.

"I think we got out of their path," said George. "Where's Mai?"

They were alone. No Captain Violet, no Miracle or Dexta or Quintalle. And no Mai.

"She probably ran back to report to her mother," said Tourmaline. "I *knew* we shouldn't have trusted her. I knew it."

George didn't contradict Tourmaline, even though he privately thought the three of them had become friends and it hadn't seemed like Mai wanted to run back to her mother at all. If she'd wanted that, she could have just done it on the beach.

"I bet she's known where my mother is all along," said Tourmaline. "I bet she knew about the magical artefacts and the source and Evelyn Coltsbody this whole time. She was just spying on us and reporting back to her mother. She probably works for the Agency herself, don't you think?"

"Tourmaline," said George. "I'm really not sure any of those things are even possible."

"I don't much care right now because I'm really angry." She breathed all the way out and slumped on to the ground, her back against a damp log. She was more than angry, she found. She was hurt, which meant that maybe she liked Mai more than she had thought she did, and that was annoying. She was secretly a little bit worried too, that her arrival on the island hadn't been the success she'd intended it to be.

She tried another long sigh to see if it would help. It didn't. "Everything's gone wrong, George."

"It's not that bad," said George, although he didn't

sound very sure. He joined Tourmaline on the ground and examined the scratches on his arms and legs.

"George, we're on our own. We can't trust anyone we've met so far. I'm tired and hungry and too hot. And … I think we might be lost. I'm supposed to be…" She sighed and leaned her head back against the log. "Maybe, for once, I should have paid attention to that sign and turned back. Everybody tried to tell me – Professor Aladeus, Josie, even you."

"But we didn't turn back," said George. "Because like you said, we're here for Persephone."

"I know," said Tourmaline quietly. "But I… I don't know what I'm doing, George."

"Neither do I," said George, rubbing at a grass stain on his sleeve. "I'm not sure anyone really does."

"Persephone *always* knows what she's doing. And *I* didn't even know that the person who's been following us ever since we left the university is Mai's mother. If she isn't Evelyn Coltsbody, then who *is*?"

"I wish I knew," said George. He patted Tourmaline's arm supportively and then hurriedly brushed an ant off his hand. "Did you notice all those bugs seemed very organized? For bugs."

"That was strange," agreed Tourmaline. "Maybe we should try to get out of this jungle, if we can."

"If we find some higher ground we'll be able to see the island better. That would help." George got up and turned in a circle. There was no path and the jungle looked the same in every direction. "Do you happen to have any idea which way we should go?"

"Don't move," said Tourmaline, very quietly. She scrambled to her feet.

There was a large and rather hairy spider crawling up the back of George's jacket.

"What? Why?" said George, instantly worried.

"Just don't move," said Tourmaline, picking up a stick.

George turned again in a panicked circle.

The spider reached his shoulder. Tourmaline grabbed George by the arm and gently flicked the spider on to the jungle floor.

"Higher ground," she said, before George could throw up or pass out, or do any of the other horror-struck things his face was threatening he might do. "You're so clever, George, and you're absolutely right –

we should get out of this jungle. Come on."

She pushed a huge leaf out of the way, ignoring the tingle of something-not-quite-right that it sent up her arm. But something shifted in the jungle. Something like a lever being thrown or a switch being pressed.

Suddenly Tourmaline's legs were scooped up beneath her. She was thrown into George, who yelped, and then they were both flung upwards, very fast and very high. There was something around them, covering them. Something sticky and familiar-feeling, but very, very wrong at the same time.

"What happened?" asked George breathlessly.

"We are caught," said Tourmaline, "in some sort of booby trap. Sorry, I think I set it off."

She looked around as much as she could, given she was squashed into a net that had snatched them up from the ground, high into the canopy of trees above.

George blew out a shaky breath and checked that he still had all his fingers. "Can you move?"

Tourmaline twisted around but only got herself more caught up in the net. "Not really, but on the bright side, we did want to get to higher ground, and this is much higher."

"It's not really what I had in mind," said George shakily.

"I know," said Tourmaline. "This is a very odd net."

She pulled at the thick webbing around them. It stuck to her hand and the more she tried to pull away, the more tangled up in it she got.

George closed his eyes for a long second. "I think it's a spider's web."

Tourmaline stopped moving. "What kind of spider makes a web like this?"

George swallowed. "A big one?"

"Well," said a voice from below. "You seem to have got yourself into quite a predicament."

Tourmaline stopped struggling and she and George locked eyes. Then they both peered down through the web to the ground but all they could see was the hazy figure of the man who'd just called up to them.

"Tourmaline Grey, I presume?" called the man.

"Who are you?"

The man laughed, a quiet, controlled laugh.

Tourmaline glanced at George. His eyes were wide

and fearful. "Can you get us down, please?" she said, her voice tight with hope.

"I think I'd prefer it if you stayed right where you are," he said.

Tourmaline squinted at the shadowy figure. It seemed familiar somehow.

George leaned forwards to Tourmaline. "How many people are on this island?" he whispered.

"Well, let's see," said the man, who seemed to have had no problem hearing George. "There's that woman from the Agency, Captain Violet's crew, you two, and, of course, me. But there aren't any inhabitants, if that's what you mean – not human ones anyway."

George shivered. "How did he even hear me?" he said, even quieter this time.

"Now that, I can answer," said the man. "I have a magical artefact on my person. One that amplifies every sound. I can hear every noise on this island and know exactly where it's coming from. It wasn't particularly difficult to wait until you two were near one of the island's many traps. In fact, I'm surprised you didn't end up in one earlier."

Tourmaline frowned. She'd seen this man before, she was sure of it. And there was someone else on this island, she was sure of that too.

"Ask him about Persephone," George mouthed at her.

"What about my mother?" she demanded. "What about Persephone Grey? She's on this island."

The man laughed again, but this time it had a harder edge to it.

Tourmaline's heart dropped back down to the ground without the rest of her.

George tried to hold Tourmaline's hand in sympathy but he couldn't find it so he squeezed her knee. "It's OK," he said. "We don't have to believe anything he says."

"You can believe whatever you like," said the man. "Just as long as you do it up there and stay out of my way. This island holds all the answers and I intend to have them."

"The answers to what?" Tourmaline demanded.

"Come on, Tourmaline. You're a clever girl, aren't you? Surely you must have noticed by now that some artefacts are special? Like that box in your professor's study. You must have known travelling around the university like that could only have been made possible by a magical artefact. When you consulted the Living Archives and got your map, you must have realized what it meant?"

"I did," Tourmaline said, then shrugged at George since she wasn't at all sure what the man meant but it seemed like a good idea to keep him talking.

"This is it, Tourmaline!" said the man. "The source of magic! It all comes from the very centre of this island, and without Persephone finding it, and without *you* trying to find *her*, I wouldn't be here right now, and it wouldn't all be mine for the taking. I suppose I should thank you for leading me here."

"You can thank me by getting us down from here," said Tourmaline.

The man laughed heartily at that. "I like you," he said. "How wonderful. Well, I really must be going. Magic to find, a world to control. Goodbye, Tourmaline. I do hope we meet again."

"Wait!" Tourmaline struggled some more. "Please, wait!"

But the man strode away and was soon swallowed up

by the jungle so that the children were alone again.

George, who had been trying to avoid letting the web touch his hair, slumped and leaned back. "So that's why Captain Violet was so keen for you to show her where this island was."

"I'm afraid we've led a lot of people here," said Tourmaline miserably.

"How does that man know so much about you?" asked George. "And how did he know about the space-between? Who is he?"

That's when all the pieces snapped together in Tourmaline's head like magnets.

"The man from Somewhere!" she cried.

George's eyebrows pulled together.

"That's where I've seen him before! And that's how he knows things – Captain Violet told him. She works for him. She put that advert in my mother's lab so we'd find it and she took us to Somewhere to tell him to follow us here. Do you remember when she was up on the balcony giving him that necklace we stole and he was staring at me? He's a collector. And clearly he's here on the island to collect all the other magical artefacts."

George frowned harder. "I think it's more than that. He wants to use the magic to control the whole world."

Tourmaline shook her head. "How? What for?"

George shrugged, as well as he could cocooned in an enormous bag of spider web. "I don't know. But I bet it's nothing good. I don't think he's a good person."

"Captain Violet said that everyone is good *and* bad."

George thought about it. "I think that's probably true. But it's like a pair of scales. You have to make sure that the good part outweighs the bad as much as you can."

They both thought about that for a while before Tourmaline quietly said, "George, it's our fault that man's here. Right after we find my mother, we have to stop him. We can't let him find the source, whatever it is."

"Definitely not," said George gravely. "But right now, what do you suggest we do?"

Tourmaline woke up with a start, still trapped in the web. George was tapping her knee furiously.

"What is it?" Her head felt stuffed full of the web they were caught in.

222

"There's something here. Below us." George's tense whisper woke Tourmaline up properly.

"What sort of something?"

"Something large. Can't you hear it crashing around in the undergrowth?"

Tourmaline listened. "You know, I'm not sure how this situation could get any worse."

"I really wish you hadn't said that," said George.

His eyes were fixed at a point above Tourmaline's head, up in the trees, and the look on his face was full horror.

George had varying degrees of horror, ranging from mild – Tourmaline had forgotten to brush her teeth, to middling – Tourmaline had put a mug of hot chocolate on top of a book and it had left a ring on the cover, to full – which she didn't see very often, but which she was looking at now.

She twisted round as best she could. At first she only saw broad green leaves and the tips of tendrils reaching up into the sky, but then her eyes locked on to many black, hairy legs, each one as long as her own.

The spider had returned.

Chapter Sixteen

Tourmaline clamped her mouth closed to bite back the scream that tried to escape, so it came out as a full-body shudder instead.

Then three things happened very quickly – the spider scuttled forwards, George screamed and Mai's face appeared over the top of the net.

"Mai!" Tourmaline struggled in the web. "How did you get up here?"

Mai was out of breath and very sweaty. "I climbed the tree. It's extremely tall. What's it like in there?"

Tourmaline blinked at her. "It's like being buried in candyfloss."

"Except that it's horrible," said George. "Can you get us out? There's a huge spider behind you."

"I'm pretending it's not there so I'm not terrified," said Mai.

"Is that working?" George asked doubtfully.

"No, not at all," said Mai, and she got out a knife.

"Wait!" said George.

"Do it," said Tourmaline.

Mai sawed through one of the four corners of the net and it dipped alarmingly, pitching Tourmaline into Mai.

"Climb over me on to the tree," said Mai through gritted teeth.

Tourmaline didn't argue. She scrambled into the foliage, clinging to a soft-barked branch. "Come on, George!"

George had his customary look of helpless terror on his face.

"You have to move!" said Mai.

"Remember back in Somewhere with Dexta's zipline?" she said. "Remember how you felt after that? You said you didn't know why you'd been scared of the Living Archives at all after you shot down that wire."

"But if I'm not supposed to be scared of this," said George, "then that implies that something worse than this is going to happen shortly afterwards."

"Just move!" said Tourmaline, who hadn't even tried to follow his logic.

The spider moved again, one of its legs twitching towards them, and George bolted out of the net, tugging his jacket from its sticky grasp, and into the tree.

The ground was startlingly far away and George could feel every inch of the distance, but it was either climb down or deal with the spider, so he climbed.

"I'm still angry with you," said Tourmaline to Mai as she looked for the next good branch.

"But thank you for rescuing us," said George pointedly as he used a thick clump of waxy leaves to anchor himself.

Tourmaline glanced at Mai and remembered that she didn't like bugs. It had been really brave to climb up the tree knowing the spider was there. Not that she was prepared to say so right then.

"You're welcome," said Mai. "But I had to really. There's no way I'm missing out on seeing how this ends."

"It's going to end with us all being eaten alive by

a giant spider if we don't get out of here fast," said
Tourmaline, making a daring leap to the ground that
knocked the breath out of her.

George followed, landing in a graceless heap.
He looked up to see Tourmaline scowling at Mai.

"Might I suggest," said George, "that we save this
until we've relocated a small distance from the giant
spider's lair?"

Tourmaline would have argued with that if she could,
but she really couldn't, so they pushed on through the
jungle with Tourmaline angrily whacking leaves out of
the way until she came to an abrupt stop.

The jungle had ended at a ravine. She stepped out on
to the strip of land between the vegetation and the sheer
drop and looked down.

"Oh dear," said George faintly.

Tourmaline sat down, her feet dangling over the edge.

Mai joined her and George opted for a seat just
behind Tourmaline, where he could grab her if for some
reason she got animated and looked likely to fall, and
also where he himself was in less danger.

"I've never seen a spider that big," said George, still

not fully recovered, but nonetheless wondering about what he'd seen so far on the island. "I wonder how it got that way."

"Maybe it's the same reason all those bugs came at us," said Tourmaline, without really thinking about it. "To stop us from—"

George was very interested in this idea, which was causing other ideas to pop inside his head, but Mai interrupted Tourmaline.

"I went back and spoke to my mother," she said quietly.

Tourmaline folded her arms. She didn't want to ask because she wanted to carry on being cross with Mai, but that lasted about three seconds before curiosity got the better of her. "And?"

Mai scooted round to face Tourmaline with a hopeful look on her face. "She's not in admin at all and she never has been! She's an undercover spy for the Agency and that's why we were at Pellavere University in the first place – the Agency had heard rumours about the Living Archives being magical and they sent her to investigate. She told me Evelyn Coltsbody collects magical artefacts and the source is how the artefacts get magical in the first place and *that's* why Evelyn Coltsbody's here! To find the source, I mean, and make a lot of magical artefacts, except my mother can't let that happen."

"We already know most of that," said Tourmaline, secretly a little bit glad that she could still be cross with Mai. "What about…?"

"Your mother?" said Mai.

"Yes," said Tourmaline. "Did she know where she is?"

Mai bit her lip and shook her head. "She didn't say anything about Persephone but she's not very happy with Captain Violet. She said she disapproved wholeheartedly of such blatant disregard for the law of the land, for decency, and for the safety of children."

Tourmaline glanced back at George, who shrugged. It wasn't an unfair assessment of the captain overall.

"Anyway," said Mai, "now the Agency are here looking for the source too."

"Is that bad?" asked George. He had a feeling that it must be because of the way Mai had said it.

Mai picked at a splinter in her palm.

"What?" said Tourmaline impatiently.

Mai sighed. "She said, 'Magic can't very well just be left out there to do as it pleases, can it?'"

"What does *that* mean?" said Tourmaline suspiciously.

"It means," said Mai, giving up on the splinter and looking plaintively at Tourmaline, "that the AICMA want to get rid of the source. And preferably the whole island."

"Get rid of?" asked George cautiously.

Mai took a slow breath. "Destroy. They want to destroy it."

"They can't do that!" cried Tourmaline. "My mother is here and – and *we're* here!"

"That's why I came back!" said Mai. "My mother is *very* protective of me. She wanted me to go back to her ship so I'd be safe and I said I would but then I ran away because I want to help you. She can't blow the island up or whatever she's planning on doing to it if I'm on it. You *have* to believe that I had no idea she was an agent. I know I should have told you it was my mother who came to the lab that day but I'm not a spy. I hope you believe me."

Tourmaline, who didn't often feel a huge amount of

sympathy for anyone other than George, felt this very keenly. "I know what it's like when adults won't tell you anything," she said. "I believe you. But are you sure you don't want to go back to her now?"

Mai gave Tourmaline a quizzical look. "Why?"

"Because you might get in a lot of trouble if you don't. This is all getting dangerous. I have to stay to find my mother but you don't." Tourmaline looked very sad for a moment. "I wouldn't blame you. If I still had my mother, I'd think about going back to her."

Mai breathed out a very long, slow breath. "She never told me there were magical artefacts until today when she absolutely had to," she said. "Never mind a magical island. And she only took the job at the university to investigate rumours about the Living Archives. So yes, I want to come with you. I didn't want to leave where I lived before and I don't like it that my mother didn't tell me the truth and I don't think anyone should go around destroying islands. I think that the world might be better with a little magic in it, don't you?"

Tourmaline smiled for the first time since they'd landed on the island. "We'd better go, then."

231

Mai got up and dusted her clothes off. "Where?"

"To the centre of the island – to the source," said Tourmaline. "My mother came here looking for it, so that's where she'll be."

Mai glanced at George. On a scale of George-being-worried, he was at about a four out of ten, so Mai nodded.

"Oh, and what does your mother look like?" asked Mai. "In case we get separated and I find her and she's unconscious, or in case you both fall into another trap and I have to fetch help and I don't know who to trust, or in case—"

"She—" Tourmaline began the sentence to cut Mai off, but then nothing else came out.

"Tourmaline?" George went up from a four to a five. Tourmaline looked as though she'd been frozen in place. Only her face moved. It twisted into an anguish that he'd never seen there before.

"What is it?" he cried. "What's the matter?"

"I can't remember what my mother looks like," said Tourmaline. "I can't remember anything about her."

Chapter
Seventeen

"My memories of my mother are fading!" Tourmaline looked so miserable that George immediately put his arms round her.

"What about everything else?" he asked. "You know who *I* am, don't you?"

"Of course I know who you are, George." Tourmaline's eyes unfocused while she searched her memories. "Everything else is there; it's just my mother. She's going away." Her voice hitched and George's heart broke a little bit.

"Maybe it's the magic," he said gently. "Maybe it's a magical artefact you touched or something. It might all come back when we leave the island."

"What if it doesn't?"

"You can't think like that," said George.

"But I *am* thinking like that," said Tourmaline. She felt as close to panic as she'd ever been. It was expanding from the inside of her chest upwards, making her teeth clamp together.

Mai was staring over the edge of the ravine, a frown on her face. "When did this start?"

Tourmaline shook her head. "I don't know. Just now?"

"No," said George suddenly. "No, it didn't. When we were on the motorcycle you forgot why you'd been to the port before."

"Did I?"

"Yes! You'd been there to wave your mother off. But you couldn't remember and I had to remind you. Do you remember that?"

Tourmaline didn't answer, which was answer enough. She was thinking about the wonderful feeling she'd had as they were sailing into the bay of Somewhere, imagining that she was adventuring just like her mother, and then the confusing feeling that followed when she couldn't remember her mother telling her about those adventures.

"So it started," said Mai, "right after you left the university."

"After," said George, as though something very terrible had just struck him, "we visited the Living Archives."

Mai frowned. "But *I* haven't lost any memories? Have you, George?"

George was just wondering how to answer that because, really, how would he know if he'd lost any memories since they'd be lost, when Tourmaline burst out, "I stepped in the pond. In the Living Archives. But it was only a tiny bit, and it was an accident."

Mai's eyes widened. "Didn't the Archive say something about paying a price if we touched the water?"

They all looked at each other.

"They can't have my memories because of a tiny accident!" said Tourmaline. "I want them back!"

"I'll go to the Archives when we get back to the university," said George fiercely, "and I'll make them give your memories back."

Tourmaline had been on the verge of tears, but

George had never said anything fiercely before and it shocked her out of it.

"I mean it," he said. "I promise I'll get them back."

Tourmaline nodded. It was a strange and troubling feeling to have missing memories. She felt sure something should be there, but she couldn't tell what, and when she reached for it, it was gone like smoke.

But if George promised something, he meant it. And although it was awful not to know what her own mother looked like, she believed him.

Then something worse occurred to her. "How am I going to find my mother if I don't know who she is? What if I see her and I don't even recognize her?"

She scrubbed her hand over her eyes, smearing dirt on her face.

"I'm here," said George. "I'll recognize her for you."

Tourmaline sniffed really hard several times.

"Come on," said Mai. "We have to find a way to the centre of the island."

She shielded her eyes against the sun. "I can't see the end of this ravine. What if it goes across the whole island? What if we climbed up to the wrong side and the centre is over there somewhere and we can't get to it?"

"That's not actually very helpful," said Tourmaline, who was now quite worried that Mai might be right.

"But," said George, "on the other hand, maybe it's a magical ravine? First it was the bugs, then it was the web trap. This isn't just any old island, is it? It's magical. And it makes the things on it magical, like the spiders. So, what if this is another trap and we just have to think of a way over it?"

Tourmaline wiped the sweat from her forehead, smearing around the dirt that was already there. "Like a bridge?"

"Bridges aren't magical," said George.

"I think they are," said Mai.

"Is any of this really helping?" asked Tourmaline.

George suddenly bent down and grabbed a handful of dirt from the side of the ravine. His face was lit with excitement.

The girls looked at each other.

"What if," said George, "there isn't really a ravine here at all? What if it's an illusion? What if it's all designed to make you think that you can't get to the centre of the island, but really, *you can?*"

On the last two words, George pulled back his arm
and flung the dirt triumphantly into the air, then less
triumphantly watched as it plummeted down into the
depths of the chasm, never to be seen again.

Mai frowned quizzically at Tourmaline. Tourmaline
shrugged.

"I really did think for a minute there," said George,
"that I was right and the dirt would fall on an invisible
pathway over the ravine."

He wiped his hand on his sleeve, almost as
disappointed about the fact that he'd got his hand dirty
for nothing. The dirt was very damp and there was now
an upsettingly muddy mark on his jacket.

"It was a nice idea," said Tourmaline. She patted
George's arm and then turned to carry on walking the
edge of the ravine. Mai followed her.

"Wait!" George hadn't moved. He was standing,
staring at his arm, which was sticking straight out over
the ravine.

"George? Are you OK?" Tourmaline hurried back to
him. "What's the matter with your arm?" He was staring

at it as though he'd never seen it before.

"It's not my arm," he said. "It's not me at all. It's my jacket. It's doing something strange."

Tourmaline exchanged a worried look with Mai, who had come to stand on the other side of George.

"Your jacket can't do things by itself, George," said Tourmaline gently. She pulled his arm down but it wouldn't move. "What are you doing?" She was stronger than George but she couldn't make his arm move even an inch.

"I told you, it's not me!" said George. "It's my jacket. Well, not my whole jacket, just the sleeve."

"Take it off!" said Tourmaline. She tugged at his other arm, pulling the jacket off him. George wriggled out of it and it hung there by the forearm of one sleeve, which was rigid and would not come down no matter what they did.

They all stared at the jacket.

"How can this – why – I don't understand," said George.

"What have you done to the sleeve?" asked Tourmaline. "Did you brush by something or touch something?"

"I haven't done anything!" said George, still staring. "No… Wait, I wiped my hand on it."

"After you threw the dirt?"

George nodded.

Then Tourmaline grabbed a handful of earth from the side of the ravine and rubbed it all over the jacket. As she did so it slowly became buoyant, like it was inflating and floating on water (except that it was floating in mid-air over a very, very steep drop).

"I quite liked that jacket," said George, a little sadly.

"You'll like it even better when we've used it to get over the ravine," said Tourmaline, thoroughly coating each shiny button with gobs of wet earth. She was trying very hard to keep the idea of her mother in her mind, but her memories were popping out of existence one by one like soap bubbles. She was desperate enough to try anything before the last memory went and she could no longer remember Persephone at all. She *had* to get to the centre of the island, and fast.

George was shaking his head increasingly fast as he realized what Tourmaline meant to do. "You can't mean that you want us to—"

"I absolutely do," said Tourmaline. "We're going to ride your flying jacket right over this ravine."

"That isn't a sentence I ever wanted to hear," said George, peering down once more into the dark.

"Perfect!" said Mai. "Like a magic carpet! Or a witch's broomstick, or a—"

"Exactly," said Tourmaline. "Now hop on and let's go!"

The jacket was now rigid, as though someone invisible were inside it, and that invisible someone could fly. The arms were stretched out on either side. Tourmaline tested the one that was over solid ground, grabbing on and hanging from it. It was a very strange feeling to be suspended in mid-air by absolutely nothing but a small and quite grubby piece of clothing.

She grasped at a memory of her mother's strong arms retrieving her from the top of the wardrobe in her bedroom. She had claimed that she wasn't at all stuck up there and could easily get down, and Persephone had said— What Persephone had said slipped away like egg white down a drain and Tourmaline grasped the jacket tighter.

"See?" she said. "It works!"

George was looking around in wonder. "My jacket has become a magical artefact!" He said the words with all the reverence he thought they deserved. Then he frowned. "But it doesn't move."

Tourmaline gave it an experimental tap forwards and the jacket bobbed gently. "If we push off I'm certain it will work."

"Like a hang glider," said Mai. "Or—"

"But there are three of us," said George.

"And it's *magic*," said Tourmaline. "Why don't you try climbing up on top of it, George? Just to see."

George looked doubtful.

"It will take your weight, I'm sure," said Tourmaline, holding out her hands in a stirrup to give him a boost.

George looked at the jacket, then back at Tourmaline, then at Mai, but she looked every bit as on board with this idea as Tourmaline.

He sighed a deeply felt sigh, and gingerly climbed on to the jacket.

"What did I tell you?" Tourmaline grinned in delight. "Mai? Now."

The girls grabbed an arm each and ran for the brink of the ravine, kicking off the edge just as George cried, "NO!"

George clutched the sides of the jacket while the girls dangled below, and it sailed onwards and upwards.

The tops of the tallest trees began to look a little smaller. Below them, they could see that the island was a strange mirror image of itself, a line of symmetry running down the middle of it like a butterfly. On both sides of the island was a brilliantly blue, sparkling sea, followed by a strip of golden sand, followed by a lush, green jungle. There was a ravine on the other side of the island too, but somehow, Tourmaline couldn't make out what the centre of the island looked like. There were clouds, or maybe a haze or a fog – something atmospheric that made her skin prickle on seeing it.

"Captain Violet!" Mai's head was twisted to the left. The captain and her crew were further along the ravine, walking the edge of it, and a little way ahead of them was Mai's mother. They all looked up at the jacket and its three passengers.

"Mai Cravenswood, come down at once!" Emiko

Cravenswood clutched at her heart and started to hurry towards the children, but she was so far away by now that it would have been impossible for her to catch them even if they had been on the ground.

Captain Violet stared up at the children in astonishment then let out a great cheer, which was taken up by the rest of the crew, except Quintalle, who looked quite sour … and also quite a lot closer than she had looked before. Tourmaline adjusted her grip. The jacket was feeling less solid than it had done. It was beginning to sink quickly. And though they'd gone impressively *up*, they hadn't made so much progress *across*, which after all had been the point in the first place.

"I think the magic is running out," said George.

"Since when does magic run out?" Tourmaline kicked her legs desperately.

"I don't know what magic does!" said George, clinging on for dear life as the jacket puttered like an engine out of fuel.

"Nearly there!" Mai was bicycling her legs as the jacket sank.

George was repeating something to himself over and over.

"What's he saying?" yelled Mai.

"A button's not scary," said Tourmaline, swinging her body back and forth to try to create some momentum.

Down on the ground ahead, Tourmaline thought she saw a black-and-white cat for a moment. One second it was there, the next it vanished. She blinked her eyes and gritted her teeth.

Mai gave one last desperate pedal, Tourmaline gave one last desperate swing, and the jacket collapsed like a balloon releasing its last dregs of air, right on the edge of the far side of the ravine.

Mai rolled on to her back, panting. The ground had never felt so good.

"George? What were you saying?"

"A button's not scary," said George. His voice was a bit muffled because his face was still pressed into the jacket and he remained curled up in a ball on top of it. "I thought if I focused on something small that was right in front of me I could avoid the crippling terror that was threatening to engulf me."

"I see," said Mai.

"I told you so," said Tourmaline, getting to her feet and brushing off some extra dirt she'd acquired. "Did anyone see what was at the centre of the island?"

"I only saw smoke or steam, or maybe gas?" said Mai.

"I thought it was clouds or fog. What about you, George?"

"Buttons," said George. "I only saw buttons."

"I thought after that zipline you realized how brave you are?" said Tourmaline.

"Yes," said George, "but I'm still *me*."

Tourmaline peered at the tendrils of mist that seemed to be moving now, something unseen pulling them down lower, amassing them in front of the children.

"What's happening?" asked Mai.

"This might sound strange," Tourmaline said, "but it's almost like the island is trying to protect itself."

"I don't think it sounds strange," said George. "In fact I think you're absolutely right. It's using whatever it can, like bugs and spiders and webs and … great, gaping chasms."

Here he had to put his head between his knees for a

second. "It's magic," he said, his voice a little muffled, "and I think it will do anything it can to stop us."

"On the bright side," said Tourmaline, whose voice didn't sound at all bright, "what's about to happen must mean we're in the right place."

Mai offered George her hand and hauled him up, just as the fog or gas or steam or whatever it was engulfed them.

Chapter Eighteen

Everything became unnaturally quiet and still. The mist hung in the air, or maybe it *was* the air. As it surrounded them and erased all sense of place and direction, they were silent.

"It's just – it's just weather," said Tourmaline eventually, her voice making George jump because he could no longer see her.

A low whistling sound began. Like wind in a tunnel. A breeze blew in their faces but the mist was dense and unmoving, which, George felt, was extremely unnerving and not at all just weather.

"Do you hear that?" Mai had her head tilted and a listening kind of frown on her face. "It's like the wind is speaking words … whispering them … or maybe—"

Suddenly the wind picked up, buffeting them back towards the chasm they could no longer see.

"Tourmaline!" The wind was whipping George's jacket (he had put it back on even though it was very dirty now) as though it was a flag. He leaned into the force.

Tourmaline couldn't tell where she was, which way was forwards or where she'd come from. George lost Mai's hand and when he called her name the wind took his voice and flung it back into his throat or took it away while laughing at him.

The mist spidered over them with damp fingers, tugging at their clothes, whispering poisonous words in their ears. George grew more and more afraid. He wanted to curl up on the ground. He wanted to go home. He wished he'd never come to the island.

The wind formed words that found their way into his mind. "You'll never be brave enough," it said. "You'll never get out of here."

Mai had called for George and Tourmaline too but no one could hear her. The words bounced back like an echo, a mocking, twisted version of her desperate cries.

"They're not your friends," hissed the wind. "They never wanted you here. You don't *have* any friends."

Mai put her head down and ran.

Tourmaline couldn't make out any words at first. The mist clung to her hair and the wind pulled at it and the words were maddeningly indistinct, but the wind repeated them over and over until she was surrounded by them and they were inside her head at the same time. "You don't know who your father is. You don't know where your mother is. Who even *are* you?" She couldn't get away from it, over and over again.

George screwed his hands into fists and took one step forwards. He wasn't sure it was forwards because the mist was everywhere but it was against the wind. And since the island wanted to stop him going the right way, it must be the right thing to do so he took it anyway.

"You can't do it," whispered the wind right inside his head.

"Yes, I can," said George, and saying it helped him believe it enough to take another step. He thought of the zipline and the climb to the island. He thought of doing what he knew was the right thing even when the adults around him seemed determined to do the wrong thing. He thought about Tourmaline and Mai, and Persephone, who had always been kind to him and who needed his help. And he thought about himself. About who he was and who he wanted to be. He didn't curl up on the ground (even though he still really, really wanted to). He walked forwards, leaning into the wind and gritting his teeth against the cold, clammy hands of the mist. He ignored its voice and he listened to the one inside himself, and that voice was telling him that he was very scared, but he was walking anyway.

Tourmaline hadn't stopped trudging into the wind since it started. It pushed her and she pushed back. If she could just get through it, she could get to her mother. Her memories had dwindled to the point of a vague sense of someone formidably clever and ferociously determined. She *had* to keep going. She *had* to find Persephone before every last bit of her was gone.

That was how Tourmaline and Mai found themselves only a short distance from one another, stumbling out of a mist that blew away into thin wisps of nothingness and a wind that died down until it was a summer's day again. They faced each other, a bit windswept and very shaken.

"I didn't enjoy that much," said Tourmaline.

"Neither did I," said Mai in a small voice. "What do you think is going to happen next?"

"It's a maze!" said George. He was in front of the girls and had kept walking even after the mist had disappeared, just to make sure. He sounded even more relieved than the time he'd been about to take the Grade Three exam on his euphonium but then the music professor had mysteriously become locked in his own music cupboard and the exam had been cancelled.

As the mist swirled and retracted like an octopus retreating into a tiny crevice, the girls caught up with George and the children stood at the mouth of a maze.

It was a maze of trees – not the palms and large, shiny green leaves of the jungle, but a dense, knotted tangle, more tightly woven than any natural wood. It still seemed to George to be the least fearsome and/or magical thing that they had yet come across. In fact, he was almost cheerful as he confidently stepped forwards, and the sight of a small, grey squirrel scampering along a branch only cheered him more. The island had tried everything it could to stop him but hadn't managed yet. Of course it couldn't have known that he was something of an expert with mazes, but he was. Jacoby had taught him.

"George!" Mai called out warningly.

"It's fine," said George. "I know exactly what to do."

It was just a matter of logic, which made George feel a lot more comfortable than he had in quite some time.

"It's easy to get to the centre of a maze," he said, turning round to face the girls and walking backwards into it. "You just keep one hand on the wall, or in this case the trees, and walk."

"It's got to be the centre of the island, hasn't it?" Tourmaline forgot how tired she was in her newfound excitement. She hadn't forgotten that she was hungry, but that couldn't be helped.

"Centre of the maze, centre of the island!" said George. "Come on!"

"It can't be that easy, can it?" said Mai, hanging back at the entrance.

"Why not?" said Tourmaline, who had been more

relieved than George to find that they were so close. Persephone was slipping away faster and faster in her mind. She wanted to believe more than anything that all they had to do was find the middle of the maze. "Hasn't this island done enough?" she said. "We deserve a bit of good luck now."

"Maybe." Mai sounded doubtful. But Tourmaline was in no mood for negativity. She stepped into the labyrinth. Mai sighed and followed and while George kept his left hand (his best one because it did all the writing) on the trees, they walked.

Down one turn, Tourmaline thought she glimpsed the black-and-white cat again out of the corner of her eye, but when she turned there was nothing but the trees, snarled and twisted together.

"What's that?" said Tourmaline suddenly. She bent down to pick something up and showed the others. On her palm was a delicate silver chain. A small locket hung from it, engraved with a star.

"Be careful," said Mai. "What's if it's a magical necklace that wants to give you an allergic reaction, or strangle you, or … I can't think of anything else."

But George was looking at Tourmaline as though he expected something from her, as though he was waiting.

"What?" she asked him. "I wasn't going to put it on or anything."

"Don't you recognize it?" he asked. He seemed excited.

She shook her head, but now she was having that feeling again, or at least the hole where a feeling should have been. It was the same not-feeling she had every time she tried to think about her mother.

"Look," he said, picking up the locket and opening it. On one side there was a tiny picture of Tourmaline when she was little, with gappy teeth and her hair in two high pom-pom pigtails. On the other side was a woman, smiling. Her hair was pulled back, but if it had been let free, it would have been in the same springy coils as Tourmaline's.

It was, in fact, a copy of the photograph that Tourmaline had stared at not so very long ago when Josie had been styling her hair. But of course, Tourmaline couldn't remember that any more.

Her chest ached with a hollow, empty feeling like it was hungry and needed filling up.

"This is a good thing, Tourmaline," said George, in his most sympathetic voice. "Persephone *must* have been here. She might be really close now! In any case, it means we're definitely on the right track."

Tourmaline stared at the tiny pictures without saying anything, and then very slowly and carefully closed the locket and put it in her pocket. Then she took a deep breath and told herself that she wasn't going to cry. "George, do you remember which way we were going? All the trees look the same to me."

"I think so," he said. "Although the whole maze looks the same."

Mai sniffed. "It wouldn't be much of a maze if it didn't."

A sound came from up in the branches. A sound that was somewhere between offended and incredulous.

"Who's up there?" Tourmaline called sharply.

"I am," said a voice, "and I don't appreciate any of you saying all trees look the same."

"But … they do," said George.

The voice made the offended sound again, louder this time. "*Some* trees are nothing more than trees. *You*, on the other hand, are currently experiencing the finest magical labyrinth the world has to offer, which you are obviously not appreciating."

Tourmaline leaned close to George. "Who is that talking?"

"I think it's that squirrel," said George, who had his eye on a squirrel – possibly the same one from earlier – who was poised on a branch above their heads.

"How incredibly stupid," said the voice. "Animals can't *speak*."

"Oh," said George, "well, of course not. I mean, not usually, but I thought—"

"Did you?" demanded the voice. "Well, I never. It thinks!"

"If it *is* a squirrel, it's a very rude one," said Tourmaline loudly.

"I'm not a squirrel!" said the voice, sounding really quite irritated now.

"Show yourself or leave us alone, then," said Tourmaline, "because we're busy."

"You're looking right at me!"

Tourmaline stared blankly into the tightly knit trees. She glanced at George. He lifted his shoulders very slightly.

"Oh for goodness' sake. I'm the majestic oak right in front of your very oblivious noses."

George snatched his hand away from the tree.

"What do you want?" asked Tourmaline suspiciously.

"What a very rude girl you are," said the tree peevishly. "I don't want anything."

"Well, we do," said George. The girls looked at him in surprise. He had a cautious but excited look on his face. The kind of look that Tourmaline knew meant he'd had a good idea.

"It's like the Living Archives!" he said, as if that explained everything. Tourmaline waited for him to actually explain everything.

"Don't you remember? The Living Archive said sort of the same thing about us being ridiculous and it reminded me what she said about trees."

Tourmaline caught on. "Yes! I remember. She said that you get one question."

She looked up at the tree. "Is that true? That we get to ask you a question? Not this one," she added hastily. "But a proper one that we think about first."

There was a pause. "I *was* going to offer to answer one question for you since it's the custom, but you've been so very difficult to deal with, I'm not sure I'm inclined."

"But you have to!" Tourmaline's mind was already spinning with possible questions.

The tree didn't answer.

George cleared his throat. "We're very sorry we were so rude."

Here Tourmaline frowned deeply and was just about to open her mouth to tell George and the tree that she wasn't rude, just tired and hungry and rather fed up with being frightened to death or covered in bugs. George saw Tourmaline's look and hastily continued, "We'd be very grateful if you answered a question for us, but if we only get one, we'd like to talk about it first."

He hoped it was enough. He'd never apologized to a tree before and wasn't sure he'd got it right.

The tree made a noise that might have been a sniff, if it had had a nose. "Get on with it, then."

They made a little huddle and put their heads close together.

"We could ask the way to the centre of the island," said Mai.

"But George already knows how to get there," said Tourmaline. "We should ask where my mother is. So we know for sure."

"Or who Evelyn Coltsbody is and what she wants?" said Mai.

"That's two questions," said George.

Tourmaline was privately wondering if she could ask how to get her mother-memory back. George thought about asking what was going to happen once they got home, then found that he didn't really want to know what an interview with his own mother was going to be like.

Mai found herself trying not to think about how she'd very much like to know if Tourmaline and George actually liked her and if they'd want to be friends when this was over. "We should ask where Persephone is," she said. "It's why we're here, after all. None of the other stuff really matters."

"You're right," said George. "Persephone is the most important thing."

Tourmaline thought about what exceptionally good friends she had, stood before the tree, put her hand in her pocket and squeezed the locket hard, then cleared her throat. "Here's our question," she said. "Where is my mother, Persephone Grey?"

Her voice came out a bit wobbly because the question felt strange when she couldn't remember who her mother was, only that she had one and she needed one and she wanted her back more than anything else in the world.

The tree shook its leaves. "Persephone Grey is at the centre of the island."

"We could have guessed that," said Mai, very, very quietly to George.

George didn't say anything, but only because he was worried that the tree would hear him, not because he didn't agree. He actually thought that she was completely right.

George and Mai might have been forming quite low opinions about trees being a waste of time altogether, but Tourmaline's heart had soared. To know that she was so close now made it feel as though all this had been worth it.

She just needed to get to the centre of the maze before her mother-memory disappeared altogether. She'd just lost her tenth birthday party, which she could have sworn had her mother in it. She had been standing next to Josie, watching Tourmaline open a present with a hopeful look on her face (it had been a large and not-at-all illustrated book about artefacts and Tourmaline had had to pretend to be grateful after a stern look from Josie).

Now when she looked up from the book in the memory, she only saw Josie, and she wondered why she had been given the book at all. Had it meant something?

She turned back to George and Mai then remembered her manners and faced the tree again.

"Thank you," she said, and because it seemed fitting that there should be something more, she gave a sort of half-bow, half-curtsy.

"This way," said George, and they turned the next corner.

All three of them stopped walking at the same moment.

From the other end of the next passageway of the labyrinth, three children stared back.

Chapter Nineteen

Several things happened very quickly. The three other children froze. Tourmaline stepped in front of George, who had been trailing his hand near to, but not on, the trees (it felt awkward touching them now that he knew they could talk). One of the other children stepped forwards and Tourmaline put her hand to her chest. The other girl did the same, confirming what she'd already realized.

"It's just us," she said. "It's a mirror."

George hurriedly stepped back out from behind Tourmaline.

"We don't look our best," said Mai, tugging a few stray bits of nature from her hair.

"Never mind that," said Tourmaline. "What's a

mirror doing in a maze?"

George looked around warily. Tourmaline ran down the path to the mirror. It was perfect – not a scratch or warp or speck of dust on it. She peered at George's reflection. "It makes you look … more real than when I actually look at you," she said.

"I don't like it," said Mai.

George was still looking around. "There's no way out," he said in dismay.

The mirror was as tall as the trees, or maybe even taller, there was no way to tell since it didn't have a frame, and it was as wide as the path in the labyrinth. Tourmaline tried to pry at its edges but she couldn't find them. The trees pushed their leaves close on either side.

The children all turned to look back the way they'd come, which was why they didn't see the George in the mirror smile a small, secret smile before he turned away too.

"We'll have to go back," said Mai.

Tourmaline pressed her hand to her forehead. "But what about George's plan to get to the middle?

I have to get to my mother right now!"

"We'll still get there," said George, looking distressed at Tourmaline's distress. "We just have to go back the way we came, turn a different way and keep turning that new way. It will still work."

The problem for George, and therefore for them all, was that his plan was founded on logic. He was perfectly right in saying he knew the best way to get to the centre of a maze. Unfortunately he was perfectly wrong in saying he knew the best way to get to the centre of a *magical* maze, which had never heard about logic and wouldn't have cared about it if it had.

They came upon mirror after mirror. The second time, mirror-Tourmaline threw her hands up in the air just a little higher than real Tourmaline and no one noticed. They stopped and turned another way every time they came to a mirror until eventually Tourmaline stuck her hands on her hips. "Stop."

"We have to keep walking," said George, "or we won't reach the middle."

"We *have* been walking," said Tourmaline, "and we're no closer to the middle than we were at the start.

Admit it, George, your plan isn't working."

George swallowed. "I don't want to," he said. "If I do that, I don't have another plan and then I don't know what to do and I don't like it when I don't know what to do. Plus, I don't want you to get upset. I want us to find Persephone."

"I know you do," said Tourmaline. "And your plan was good. But it isn't working any more because of the mirrors. We have to stop and make a new one."

Mai sat down on the ground. She thought she might as well.

Tourmaline cleared her throat. "Excuse me? Trees? Could we ask another question, please?"

She waited but although a few leaves ruffled themselves, there was no answer.

"What now?" asked Mai.

"Well," said Tourmaline. She had been trying to force her brain to work like George's because her own was getting very tired and starting to feel hopeless. "There are only two things in this labyrinth," she said slowly. "One of them is trees, and the other is mirrors, and the trees won't help us." She said this last part a little more forcefully than the rest and matched it with a scowl directed at one or two branches.

"Do you think the mirrors will?" asked George. He had sat down too and was pulling the tiny bobbly bits off his socks, though it wasn't going to make him look any tidier.

Mai was still trying to get rid of the idea the wind had pulled out of her head – that the other two didn't really like her as much as she wanted them to. "They're doing the opposite so far," she said.

Tourmaline sat on the ground too, then when that didn't help, lay down and stared up at the sky. The mist had now formed itself into well-behaved clouds and she watched them and wished that she had a thick slab of jam sponge, or even a small triangular sandwich, because this would all be a lot easier if she weren't hungry.

Mai lay down too and tried to think of something useful, which was made difficult by the fact that she was starting to fall asleep.

Suddenly Tourmaline pushed herself up on to her elbows, and then on to her hands.

"What is it?" Mai scrambled up too.

Tourmaline was looking around, at first alert and then with growing alarm.

"Where's George?"

George was gone.

Tourmaline had run through the maze with Mai following, calling out George's name, her hands sweaty, her stomach in twists, until she was thoroughly lost and completely certain that, somehow, George was gone.

She and Mai sat quietly by another mirror, or maybe it was the same one, she had no idea.

"This is all my fault," said Tourmaline miserably. "I keep losing people and even when I'm supposed to be finding someone, I lose someone else. And it's *George*."

Mai tried to remember that Tourmaline was upset and ignore that it sounded as though she would much rather it had been Mai that had disappeared.

"We'll get George back," she said, even though they had no clue where he'd gone.

Tourmaline kicked the ground.

Mai bit her lip. "I know it's not the same as having

George here, but I'm with you."

"It's not that," said Tourmaline. "It's just … you don't know my mother. George is the only one left who does." She felt utter dejection right down into her toes, so she kicked the ground again. "George was supposed to recognize my mother for me so the island's taken him away."

Mai's eyebrows shot up. "You have the locket! That's how you'll know your mother when you find her." She was relieved to have thought of at least one small thing that was helpful.

Tourmaline stood up and eagerly dug in her pocket, then in another, and another while her face changed from hopeful to not hopeful at all. "It's gone," she said. "I've lost it, so that's no help." She was close to tears but sometimes that made her angry and this was one of those times.

Mai turned herself so that she was facing away from Tourmaline and put her arms rigidly round her knees. Tourmaline looked at her for a moment and then set her jaw. She had to do *something*, even if she wasn't sure what. *What would Persephone do?* she asked herself. What would her doubtless brave and probably handsome and definitely tall father do?

He was probably a genius. He probably worked out problems like this before breakfast and then got on with his real work as a famous animal surgeon or mountaineer. He probably came up with so many brilliant solutions he couldn't use them all and tossed them out like orange peel.

She thought about what she and George and Mai had been talking about right before George disappeared. Something about how there were only trees and mirrors, and the trees were no help.

She walked up to the mirror, glanced over her shoulder at Mai, who was still staring resolutely in the opposite direction, and said, "Let me pass! Please."

Then, "Can you move?"

And after that, "Show us the path to the centre of the maze."

The mirror didn't move.

Tourmaline scowled, snatched up a piece of gravel and threw it at the mirror. Something, somewhere, deep inside the reflection, wavered like the flicker of a candle, and the gravel disappeared. Tourmaline peered closer. The reflection looked so very real. More real than a reflection had any right to look.

Suddenly she noticed George in the reflection, way back at the end of the path. She swung round but the path behind her was empty. There was only Mai sitting on the grass. She turned back to find George in the mirror. He tilted his head and beckoned her with one finger.

Tourmaline glanced over her shoulder. No George. And when she turned round again to the mirror, or whatever it was, he had turned round in there too and was running away from her.

She put out her hand and tapped the mysterious surface. Her finger went straight through, like she'd pushed it into jelly. Her heart lurched up so high it felt like it was banging against her collarbone. She put her hand on the flat surface and pushed. It went right through. "George!"

He was almost gone, so she stepped forwards quickly. And instead of banging into glass, she walked *into* the mirror, like passing through a waterfall and coming out on the other side. The surface moved around her like liquid metal and then back into place.

She hadn't noticed the smile on the face of the mirror-Tourmaline just before she went through it.

In front of her it was darker than it had been before. Not like night, but a strange, silent dusk. The trees were gone. The maze was gone. George was gone.

She turned round and shouted out to Mai. But she was gone too. The mirror wasn't there any more. She spun in a circle. What had she done?

There was nothing in the strange mirror-world. It was as though all colour and sound had been leached out of it. She stood there for several seconds, not knowing what to do, but there was only one path and it was in front of her. Which, she thought, made things easier, choice-wise. She walked forwards, trying to think of the mirror-space as something like the space-between at the university, and then she started to run, firstly because the place she was in was as quiet as a graveyard and as cold and miserable too, and secondly because she had thought to herself, what if the mirror-space *was* like the space-between? What if it led to the place she wanted to go? To the middle of the labyrinth?

But the path just kept going and nothing changed, however fast she ran. Was Persephone trapped somewhere like this, just like she was, running nowhere endlessly, for all time? No – the trees might be infuriating but she didn't think they were liars, and they'd said Persephone was at the centre of the island.

But what about George? Why had he run away from her, and where was he now? The thought that he might be gone forever made her breathe too quickly and then too slowly, like she couldn't manage even that properly if he wasn't with her. She should have been out of breath by now. She *was* out of breath but somehow she couldn't hear it. She thought perhaps it was best not to think about that too much. Like a lot of the things that had happened recently.

She stopped running. Then started again. Then stopped again. She looked back the way she had come. Then in front, the way she had been going. Then she looked up, and down, just to be sure. There was only the path.

And the nothing that wasn't the path.

But she had tried that way and it hadn't worked, so she tried the nothing. She closed her eyes and put out one foot and stepped forwards (and might even have let out a very un-Tourmaline-like, much more George-like, squeak if she'd been able to). Her foot landed and light hit her face.

She opened her eyes (it probably hadn't been necessary, she thought now, to close them), and there it was. Another mirror, or barrier, or whatever, with a bright sunlit scene on the other side of it. It was right in front of her. The centre of the maze. A large octagonal clearing, the walls made of trees densely twisted together.

She let out a relieved shout that made no noise at all. But, oh, how she wished George and Mai were there with her.

Tourmaline screwed her hands into fists and stepped out of the mirror. She didn't see the girl behind her, the girl who looked just like her, reaching out a hand to grab her, brushing the ends of her curls with her fingers just before she escaped.

The moment her foot touched the grass, sound returned. She realized how very strange it was when it wasn't there and how very loud it was now that it had come back.

She also realized someone was in the centre of the maze already. He stopped and stared at her and she stared back. It was him. The man who had stared so intensely at her when Captain Violet had given him the stolen necklace. The man who had left them in the spider's web. The man who probably worked for Evelyn Coltsbody. He was at the centre of the island and he'd got there first.

Tourmaline turned round but there was nowhere to run and besides, there was no way she could leave her mother now that she was so close. The trees had said Persephone was at the centre of the island and this was it. She was here. Even if Tourmaline couldn't see her.

The man laughed an astonished laugh that was loud after the silence inside the mirror. He stepped closer. Tourmaline stepped back.

"Tourmaline! You really are a resourceful girl. Not that I'm surprised."

Tourmaline swallowed.

"I had no idea you were coming." He pulled

something from his pocket. It was a shell, smooth and creamy pink – the kind you can hear the sea in. "This is the magical artefact I told you about. It lets me hear everything on the island but I suppose it doesn't work if you're using a mirror to travel." He put the shell back in his pocket. "And what are you planning to do now?"

There was no way Tourmaline was going to tell him that. None at all. Except that her gaze wandered around the clearing, looking for Persephone. Was she hiding in the trees?

"I see," he said. "So it's the magic you're after."

Tourmaline shook her head.

"No?" said the man.

He pulled something else out of his pocket and held it up. It was a pocket watch, a rather fine gold one, if somewhat large and old-fashioned. As the man pressed a button on the side of the watch, Tourmaline made a run for it. And something very strange indeed happened.

Chapter Twenty

Tourmaline stopped running. Not because she wanted to but because she *had* to. She was frozen in place, completely unable to move. Her arms and legs wouldn't budge, no matter how hard she tried.

"Let me go!" she shouted, glad to find that her voice still worked.

The man sighed. "It won't be so bad, Tourmaline. I'll simply control all the magic in the world. I promise there'll be barely any changes at the university. Oh, maybe Professor Aladeus will be dean instead of Faiza Gramercy, and I daresay there'll be a few dismissals after that, but I assure you, I intend to be the very picture of kindness and benevolence when everything belongs to me."

Tourmaline was panting with the effort of trying to move. "What does Professor Aladeus have to do with anything? I'm here for my mother!"

"Did you think," he asked her, with the air of a cat toying with a mouse, "that the mirror-world was a little like what happens when you use the magician's box?"

Tourmaline stared at the man in shock. That was almost exactly what it had felt like in the mirror-world. Come to think of it, the Living Archives had that same sense of unreality too. The idea of it all being linked burst in her head like on an overripe berry. "How did—?"

He smiled widely. "So you *did* use it, then. Who do you think gave Professor Aladeus that box?"

He paused, one eyebrow raised, looking pleased with himself. "*I* gave it to him to help me gather the information I needed."

Tourmaline's mouth opened and closed while she thought about the entrance to the space-between that was in her mother's lab. If she could have kicked herself for not going back to find out where it led – undoubtedly to the magician's box – she would have.

"But that box has been there for years!" she said at last, giving up her attempts to move.

"And those years have been worth it in the end." The man raised his arms to indicate the island around them. "Persephone got close so many times, but this time, *this* time, Tourmaline, she finally did it. Your mother found the Source of all magic." (That was how he said it, as though the word was capitalized.)

"And Professor Aladeus told *you*?" Tourmaline couldn't convey her rage properly since she had no choice but to stay perfectly still, so she worked very hard at putting it all into her voice.

The man just laughed. "Well, it's what I paid him for. He wouldn't have been much of a spy otherwise. But anyway, it was you who led me here in the end. You've been much more use than he ever was."

Suddenly Tourmaline remembered Captain Violet saying it had been a group effort to get her aboard *The Hunter*. And the Living Archives saying someone else had been bothering them. Professor Aladeus.

After her mother had vanished and everything she'd done to find her, only to lose both her memories and her best friend in the whole world, after all that, this … this *terrible* man was making everything worse. Tourmaline was angrier than she'd ever been before.

"What are you even going to *do* with all the magic?" she yelled.

The man looked up at the sky and rocked back on his heels. "There are a lot of people who will pay a lot of money for a magical artefact, Tourmaline. And when I control the Source, I can make as many artefacts as I like. Did you know there's a story about an artefact whose owner can make you believe anything they say? I intend to find that particular treasure." He looked across the clearing to where the maze led away on the other side. "Very shortly, in fact. Maybe I'll make myself the ruler of Escea. And why stop there? I've always liked the Midnight Islands. I could own them! Would you like that?"

"Why would I like that?" yelled Tourmaline. She couldn't seem to stop shouting. "You're worse than Emiko Cravenswood and Captain Violet and – and Evelyn Coltsbody all rolled into one! Who are you and why are you doing all this? Where are my friends?

Where's my mother?"

At that, the man laughed and laughed. He even wiped his eyes when he'd finished. "I can't deny it's true that I'm a lot of things," he said. "For example, I'm not working for Evelyn Coltsbody, I *am* Evelyn Coltsbody." He shook his head. "Didn't Captain Violet tell you any of this? Why did you think she brought you to Somewhere? It wasn't just so I could follow you to Elsewhere, it was because I was curious to finally see you. And see if you had any propensity to follow in my footsteps. It seems that you do, judging by the gusto with which you took part in the necklace heist."

Tourmaline stared at him. A strange, cold tingle tiptoed from the back of her head to the tip of her nose. "What do you mean, follow in your footsteps?" she asked cautiously.

The man looked back at her steadily. "I'm your father, Tourmaline."

If Tourmaline hadn't already been frozen, she wouldn't have been able to move anyway. She couldn't move, she couldn't speak, she didn't even blink.

"Anyway, obviously there's nothing here and this

maze is just another one of the island's defences. It's quite remarkable, don't you think? But I must be getting on," said Evelyn Coltsbody. "Good luck, my dear." He smiled and turned and walked away across the clearing and back into the maze.

Chapter
Twenty-one

Tourmaline stared after him as he disappeared back into the trees. She wasn't sure, but she thought her heart might have been frozen along with the rest of her. She hadn't rescued her mother: all she'd done was lose George and Mai. She hadn't stopped the island from falling into the hands of the worst man in the world, and the worst man in the world – Evelyn Coltsbody – was her *father*.

But that last part couldn't be true. It just couldn't be. He wasn't brave, he wasn't kind, and now she could see him properly he wasn't even that tall. Of all the fathers that Tourmaline had dreamed up over the years, he was none of them. And she was nothing like him. Was she?

Just at that second, Mai burst out of the mirror and stumbled on to the ground.

She scrambled to her feet, shouting, "You can't have the magic! We're here to save Tourmaline's mother!" and finally, "Stop!"

The man didn't stop. He'd already gone.

Mai stared at Tourmaline. "There's a Mai in there but it's not me. *I'm* the only me who's me. And I had to run so fast. Tourmaline, it was the worst—"

"Mai," said Tourmaline. "Help."

"Right." Mai ran over to Tourmaline. She kicked something on the way, something that had been dropped on the ground. It was the pocket watch. She picked it up by its chain.

"Do you think it can undo—"

"Just try it!" said Tourmaline.

Mai pressed the side of the watch and the hands started ticking around again and Tourmaline, suddenly released from the magic, fell on to the grass.

"Are you all right?" asked Mai. She bit her lip. "I saw everything. I would have come out sooner but—"

"It's OK," said Tourmaline. Were her lips numb?

She thought they might be. They felt very strange, like the rest of her. "If you'd come out he'd have frozen you too."

She rested her arms on her knees and her head on her arms and concentrated very hard on not crying.

"Tourmaline."

Tourmaline sighed but didn't move.

Mai tapped the back of her head. "Tourmaline? Something has happened and I think you need to see it."

Tourmaline's head snapped up and she looked across the maze to where Evelyn Coltsbody had disappeared.

"Not there," said Mai. She pointed. "There."

Tourmaline made a noise that was part cry of delight and part shocked gasp.

Inside the mirror, there were two Georges.

One had the other in a headlock, and the other was pinching the arm round his neck and squirming. When they saw the girls looking, they both straightened up guiltily and started talking, pointing at each other.

Mai went to stand in front of the mirror. The two Georges were conducting a lively argument but the girls couldn't hear a word of it.

"Which one is our George?" Mai peered closely at the two boys. They were absolutely identical, from the scratches on their legs to the dirt on their faces.

Tourmaline shook her head, staring from one George to the other.

One boy shoved the other, and the other looked indignant and then started an angry-looking tirade that went on for quite some time.

"What shall we do?" Mai asked Tourmaline, since neither of them could hear a word either boy said.

One of the Georges tapped on the mirror then pointed at Tourmaline.

"What does he want?" asked Mai.

"I don't think he can get out," said Tourmaline.

"You can't get out?" she mouthed at the mirror in an exaggerated way.

George shook his head. George II shook his head as well. Then they both mimed a pulling motion and put their hands out towards Tourmaline.

"I can pull you out?"

The Georges nodded. Both put their hands to the mirror. Then they scowled at each other and began arguing again, each pointing to his own chest then turning to Tourmaline to convince her which George was the correct George.

"Why can't they just step out?" asked Mai.

"Do we want them to?" asked Tourmaline.

"Good point," said Mai as she shivered. "I wouldn't want the mirror-Mai out here. Maybe they're both trapped because we have to pick the right one to bring out?"

"What happens if I get the wrong one?"

The Georges suddenly stopped arguing and turned to Tourmaline again.

"Which one do I choose?" Tourmaline said. She tried to say it out of the side of her mouth so that Mai would hear, but George – her George – wouldn't be offended that she couldn't tell him from the magical imposter.

Then one George frowned. It was the frown of a George thinking deeply about something. He took a small step back. He looked at the other George (who still seemed to be putting forth a brilliant argument about why he was the one who should be pulled through the mirror) then he looked right at Tourmaline and sadly shook his head.

"What's he doing?" said Mai.

Tourmaline frowned. "I don't know."

The sad George took a step back from the surface of the mirror. He pointed at the girls and made a shooing motion.

Tourmaline frowned deeper. "I think he might be saying that if we can't tell which George is the right one, we should leave them both in there and carry on without him."

"Oh," said Mai. "But what if our George gets lost in there forever? Or what if we pull them both out? Then we might be able to tell which one is ours. Do you think that would be bad? Or maybe we could—"

"I know which one is my George," said Tourmaline suddenly. She reached through the mirror, her fingers breaking the surface as though it were a very still pond, grabbed the sad shooing George and pulled him through. He came out gasping and patted himself all over as though he were making sure he was real. She flung her arms around him and hugged him hard enough that it almost hurt.

He hugged her right back, almost as fiercely. "How did you know it was me?"

Tourmaline pointed back into the mirror. The other George now wore an expression that the real George would never have – one of angry malice. "Because you, George," she said, "are a good person, really and truly, and as soon as you said that I should leave both Georges in the mirror just in case the wrong one got out, I knew you were the right one."

"Here," said George. He handed Persephone's locket back to Tourmaline. "I found this."

Tourmaline opened the locket and drank in the tiny picture of her mother. It hurt her heart and helped it, both at the same time. She closed her fingers around the locket. "Thank you, George. It's lovely to have this back, but it's even better to have you."

George looked into the mirror. Mirror-George smiled spitefully and stalked away back into the silent mirror-world. "I am very, *very* glad that you picked the right me."

Tourmaline looked at her friend as he watched his other self disappear. "What happened in there?"

George shook himself slightly. "One day I'll tell you. But not today. Where's Persephone? Isn't this the centre of the island?"

Mai gave a helpless shrug. Tourmaline looked at the ground. Everything that had just happened was churning in the back of her mind, but she'd been happy to leave it there while they dealt with the problem of two Georges.

"Tourmaline?"

Looking at the ground hadn't been enough. She suddenly felt the need to lie down on it, so she did, her arms and legs spread out like a dejected starfish.

"Give her a minute," said Mai quietly. She tilted her head at George and after they'd walked a few paces away, she told him, in hushed tones, that they hadn't found Persephone, that they hadn't yet found the centre of the island after all, and that the mysterious man who, it seemed, had been one step ahead of them since the very beginning, was Evelyn Coltsbody. She hesitated to tell George he was also Tourmaline's father but when she faltered, Tourmaline caught her eye and nodded, so Mai took a deep breath and explained.

George blinked several times then went over to Tourmaline. She sat up with an effort, and he put his arms round her. Like a lot of people, Tourmaline felt that when someone was kind to her, she was all the more likely to cry, and that's exactly how she felt at that moment. A hard, painful lump had somehow wedged itself into her throat and her eyes stung with tears.

"He's not a brave adventurer," she said, although it was hard to hear her.

"Maybe not," said George. "But *you* are."

Tourmaline sniffed hard. George wondered if she was going to cry, and if so, was anything going to come out of her nose (he had a particular aversion to that sort of thing and he didn't want it on his jacket, even though the jacket was now well beyond saving). Then he decided that nothing really mattered as much as Tourmaline did, and squeezed her a bit tighter.

After a long moment, Tourmaline sighed and lay back down. It wasn't very comfortable. In fact, there was something digging into her back. But she didn't deserve to be comfortable. Persephone probably wasn't, wherever she was. She wished, with an aching sense of

emptiness in her chest, that she could remember
her mother. At the moment, the only parent she
could bring to mind was a man she only knew a very
little about, and she didn't like that little bit at all.
She squirmed in her own skin, and it was only partly
to do with the lump sticking into her back.

Mai sat down next to George, who was fretting with
the end of his shoelace and casting worried glances at
Tourmaline. The fretting and the casting continued
as the minutes ticked by until Mai reached out to bat
George's hand away from his shoe and Tourmaline
moved at last.

"You know," she said, "the island has just been one
thing after another. First the bugs and then the webs and
the chasm and the mist and the maze and the mirrors."

"We know," said Mai.

"We were there," said George.

"But then," said Tourmaline, as though she
were slowly working something out. "That man…
Evelyn Coltsbody went back into the maze. But the
whole island is defence after defence designed to
stop us getting to the centre. I think he was wrong.

We've already beaten the maze."

George and Mai exchanged a quick look as Tourmaline reached underneath her back to find the thing that was digging into her (she didn't deserve to be *that* uncomfortable), and as she felt the shape of what it was that had probably left a bruise by now, a very important realization came loose from – or flew into – her head.

She shot bolt upright.

"I'm right," she said.

"About what?" asked George, who had been waiting anxiously for some kind of decision.

Tourmaline smiled her most triumphant smile. "I've discovered something important. We don't have to go to the centre of the island, we have to go to the *centre* of the island!"

"Great!" said George. "Wait, what?"

Chapter Twenty-two

"What do you mean, the *centre* of the island, not the centre?"

Tourmaline beamed jubilantly and pointed at the ground in front of them. Mai looked bemused for a few seconds before her face lit up with understanding. "We have to go underground? What, like climb down a well, or a mine, or a— Oh! Down that chasm we flew over."

Tourmaline brushed the grass and stray leaves away from the uncomfortable thing that she had been lying on and found exactly what she thought she would. It was a rusty iron ring, thick and black and cold. She crouched over it while George and Mai made gratifying sounds of wonder and excitement, and pulled on it.

The grass around it made a ragged, tearing sound as the hatch came open. Cold, musty air filled a dark space where worn stone steps descended into the earth.

Tourmaline shrugged. "We could just take these stairs."

George shook his head, though he was almost smiling. "You're starting to sound like you really belong here. But if I had to choose between a chasm and some stairs, I think we all know which one has my vote."

"I feel as though I kind of understand this place now," said Tourmaline. "So let's go. And bring that." She pointed to the pocket watch that was still in Mai's hand.

Mai looked down at it. "Do you – do you want me to come? You can just take the watch if you like."

Tourmaline looked confused for a second. It seemed as though Mai really wanted to come with her and George, though she wasn't looking at Tourmaline properly. Then Tourmaline remembered that she hadn't always been the kindest person in the world when it came to Mai. She thought about how she'd acted just before she'd gone into the mirror and wondered how she could have been such a brat. Mai had done nothing but help, even when she'd had to ignore her own mother to do so.

"Of course you should come," said Tourmaline. "You're our friend and we need you there. If you want to."

"Of course I want to," said Mai. "You're *my* friends. And I want to help find Persephone."

Tourmaline nodded firmly. "You keep the pocket watch. What else have we got?"

She dug in her pocket, her fingers first moving over and then stopping on Persephone's locket. She didn't pull it out to show the others. She didn't want the annoying lump in her throat to come back. Not now.

"I don't have anything," said George, looking as though he wished he had a sword to defend them all, or at the very least a sandwich.

"That's not true," said Tourmaline. "You have the best brain of anyone I know, and that's not nothing."

George smiled, a little faintly. "I take it everywhere with me."

"Good," said Tourmaline as she put her foot on the first step. "I have a feeling we're going to need it."

They crept down the steps in the dim light until Mai suddenly stopped. "Wait!"

George jumped.

"We have to close the hatch behind us," said Mai.

George shook his head. "It'll be pitch black."

"If *he* comes back, he'll follow us," said Mai. "And so will Captain Violet, and if my mother gets through the maze, she *definitely* will."

"She's right," said Tourmaline, already running back up to close the hatch.

George pressed himself against the damp earth wall and closed his eyes. Then he opened them in case of imminent attack.

None came. But it was very dark. Which was, he told himself, why he screamed when something brushed his hand.

"It's only me," said Tourmaline, a little breathlessly. "Both of you, hold my hands. And try not to think about anything in particular."

George looked almost offended, although Tourmaline

couldn't see it. "Tourmaline, I can't possibly—"

"George, you have to trust me."

She took his hand firmly, found Mai, and led them both down the steps.

She'd been thinking about the island more and more and she'd decided that it wasn't a matter of the place being difficult for the sake of it. It wasn't trying to stop her from rescuing her mother. It was behaving this way for a reason – as things or people who are labelled difficult often are – and that reason was to protect the Source of magic. Every time they got close, the island had done something to stop them.

So she came at the problem sideways, as you might do with a skittish cat, walking almost carelessly (as much as she could when making her way down steps in the dark), trying to think of other things.

And in that way they walked right to the bottom of the steps. Where they ended a tunnel began, like a large mineshaft, tall enough for even Mai to walk upright.

"I can see!" said George.

There was dim light, a glowing phosphorescence coming from seams in the rock and George, for one, was extremely glad of it.

A black-and-white cat suddenly appeared in front of them and he grabbed Tourmaline's arm. "Where did that come from?"

The cat made an inquisitive noise and blinked its yellowy eyes. Its paws were placed neatly in front of it facing outwards as though it were a ballet dancer waiting to begin. It stared hard at Tourmaline, then turned tail (elegantly) and began to trot away.

"Should we follow it?" asked Mai doubtfully, as the cat broke into a run. "It could be one of the island's illusions. It could be a cat-shaped trap."

"I don't know," said George. "I've seen it somewhere before."

"So have I," said Mai, "but that doesn't mean it isn't a—"

"We don't have time to discuss it," said Tourmaline, and took off after the cat. "My mother is right here and I *have* to find her."

George looked at Mai and Mai looked at George, and they both ran after Tourmaline, who was dashing along the tunnel.

"This cat looks," said George, slightly out of breath now, "an awful lot like a cat we used to have at the university. But that cat disappeared."

The cat darted to a turn in the tunnel, and maybe it had heard what George said, because it suddenly vanished from sight.

Tourmaline dashed after the cat. Even though she'd only just looked at the picture of Persephone in the locket, the image had become fuzzy already. She was losing her very last memory of her mother. She screwed her hands into fists to try to keep hold of it as she turned the corner.

"Where did it—?"

They all stopped. A vast cavern opened up in front of them. It was as though the centre of the island was hollow and Tourmaline had the strange feeling of being inside a vast chocolate Easter egg.

Mai tilted her head. She could hear running water.

"Oh," said George. He said it very quietly and his voice echoed very quietly.

Tourmaline had put her hands out, stopping Mai on one side of her and George on the other from rushing forwards.

There was a woman kneeling on the ground on the far side of the cavern. Luminous rocks were piled in front of her. She seemed to have been writing something but when she saw the children, she stopped and stood up. A sheaf of papers dropped from her hand and hit the ground with a rustle. A moment of silence followed.

"Careful," Tourmaline murmured to the others.

George gently pressed Tourmaline's arm down and tugged her forwards a few steps. "Tourmaline." He sounded sad. "Hello, Persephone," he said, louder and more deliberately, still leading Tourmaline forwards.

"Tourmaline?" said Persephone. She took a step towards her daughter, then ran and threw her arms round her.

"Oh," said Tourmaline.

Persephone wrapped her arms round Tourmaline so tightly that she couldn't breathe. They were very nearly the same height and Tourmaline could feel her mother's heart beating against her own, which felt brittle enough to crack into a million porcelain pieces. She had never felt so unspeakably sad.

She lifted her head from her mother's shoulder and caught George's eye.

George's hands were clasped and his eyebrows were pulled together in anxiety. He was clearly waiting to see if Tourmaline remembered something. Anything.

A tear tracked down her cheek. She blinked, desolate.

She remembered nothing.

Tourmaline slowly raised her hand and, as her mother held her, pressed her finger to her lips.

George looked at Mai, and they both nodded.

Persephone suddenly let go, holding Tourmaline at arm's length. "Oh my goodness, what am I doing? You have to leave! Right now."

"Yes," said Tourmaline hurriedly. "We should leave. We came to rescue you."

"Thank you. That was very brave," Persephone's voice was a wonderful mix of pride and marvel. Then she gathered up the children as though she were a sheepdog and herded them quickly back towards the tunnel they'd just exited. "But you have to go."

Tourmaline was just about to ask why her mother had said "you" and not "we", when it started.

A sound, an unmistakeable sound, was coming from down the tunnel, getting closer by the second.

"Oh no," said Persephone.

Chapter Twenty-three

A howling wind screamed towards Persephone and
the children, raging down the tunnel, tearing out into
the cavern and sweeping up everything in its path.
Tourmaline's curls were blasted forwards as she was swept
off her feet and blown, the tips of her toes dragging on the
ground, all the way across the huge cavern.

She was breathless and dishevelled by the time
the wind dropped her, the noise of it still rushing in
her ears.

She spun round to find that George had gone full
turtle, curled up into a ball with his hands over his
ears and his eyes screwed shut. Mai was wide-eyed
and out of breath and Persephone's hair was wild.

"Is everybody OK?" Persephone asked, pushing curls

out of her eyes.

"What *was* that?" asked Mai, as George uncurled.

"That," said Persephone, "was the island. I thought if I could get you out quick enough…"

She broke off and closed her eyes and the look on her face alarmed George so much, he got up and burst out, "What? What is it, Persephone?"

Persephone sat down heavily on the ground. "I've been stuck in this cavern ever since I found the Source," she said. "I think I must have been the first person in a long time to find my way through the island's defences. They only exist to protect the Source and now I've found it, the island won't let me leave."

She looked at the children, her dark eyes so sad that George took hold of Tourmaline's hand.

"And now it won't let you leave either," she said.

The rushing sound got louder. They couldn't be trapped. Tourmaline couldn't have gone through everything she'd gone through on the island and lost her very last memory of her mother the second before she found her … and after all that, not even be able to rescue her.

"No," she said. She was shaking her head. "No, we *have* to get out of here. We came here to rescue you and—"

She stopped so suddenly, George squeezed her hand. "The island won't let her go," she said.

Mai looked between Tourmaline and George for answers.

George sighed. "It's what the Living Archive said. Tourmaline asked him how an island could stop a person from leaving it, and he said—"

"You'll find out, once it's too late," Tourmaline finished quietly.

They all sat or stood and blinked and sighed.

"Wait," said Persephone, "you went to the Living Archives?"

Tourmaline cast a fearful glance at George. He understood that she didn't want to talk to her mother about the Living Archives and what had happened to her memories because of it.

"What's that noise?" he said quickly.

Tourmaline frowned. She could hear it too, and now she realized that it wasn't the wind still in her ears or even blood rushing around in her head; it was a nearby waterfall, plunging down, impossibly fast and impossibly far and just … impossible.

Tourmaline took a tentative step forwards and looked down over a precipice that dropped deep into a fathomless pool roiling with colour like oil on water. Mai joined her, and George inched closer.

"Does that look … familiar to you?" Tourmaline asked them.

Both George and Mai nodded.

"It's like the pond at the Living Archives, isn't it?" she said. "Except … more."

"More," George echoed faintly.

"It's the same substance," said Persephone. "This is the Source."

"You really did find it, then," said George.

Persephone's quick brown eyes settled on him and she smiled sadly. "I really did. I'd been hunting it so we could renew the water at the Living Archives. Not that it's water, of course, not really."

"No," said George. "It's not water at all. But it sort of acts like it, doesn't it? I mean, all the trees growing there are steeped in it, aren't they? And the books, and ... and the Living Archives themselves, in a way. And then the professors and the students, they all use the books and the knowledge and – and *that's* why the university is the best in the country, isn't it? It's all because of the magic."

"Very good, George," said Persephone, smiling warmly and looking a little more like her old self. "But the magic is wearing thin and it's not as predictable as it once was. Hence my current mission, at which I seem to be failing quite spectacularly."

"There has to be a way out," said Tourmaline, who hadn't been listening and had other concerns on her mind. "We can beat the wind if we run fast enough."

Persephone sighed. "It won't work."

Mai and Tourmaline exchanged a look and started running at the same time.

Only to be buffeted right back to where they had started by the wind, which suddenly picked up out of nowhere.

George had watched, wide-eyed, and now he turned, still wide-eyed, to Persephone. "But we can't stay here," he said.

"I'm hungry," added Mai.

"Are we going to starve?" said George, a note of hysteria entering his voice. His eyes had gone very round and Mai's hand had moved unconsciously to her stomach.

Persephone said very firmly, "Nobody is going to starve."

She pulled an apple out of one of her pockets, took a bite out of it, then carefully attached it to a hook on a thin skein of what looked like fishing line that she'd tucked neatly into a breast pocket.

George glanced at Mai, and Mai widened her eyes and shrugged, as Persephone carefully leaned over the Source and lowered the apple into it.

Seconds later, she pulled it back up and George gasped.

The apple was whole again, its smooth pink skin unbroken.

"I've had quite some time to study the Source," said Persephone, unhooking the apple and offering it to Tourmaline, who turned it around in her hands.

"It really is fascinating. Obviously we knew from the books in the Living Archives that objects could become magical on contact with the Source, but I never suspected that the particular type of magic might be linked to the nature of the item *before* it ever became magical."

George blinked and a slow smile of understanding spread across his face. "Like the rope!" he said.

Persephone's eyebrows quirked a question.

"We climbed up here using a magical rope," said Mai.

Persephone nodded. "Exactly! Rope is for climbing. It probably belonged to someone who found the island long ago. The rope came into contact with the Source, and the Source simply enhanced its ropeness.

"It's just lucky I had an apple with me when I found the cavern," she added. "I am rather sick of apples, though."

Persephone's eyes were shining now. She was acting much more like she usually did. "You should see what's happened to the other items I had in my backpack." She frowned. "But of course, I can't really explain the cat."

311

George noticed the change in Persephone but Tourmaline couldn't, because she no longer had any idea what Persephone was usually like. "I can't explain my jacket either," he said.

"Your jacket?"

"I think that might be a story for later," said George. "But the cat, it's from the university, isn't it?"

Persephone nodded.

"I knew I'd seen it before!"

"Your mother's favourite," she said. "She even had her portrait painted with it. She was quite upset when it disappeared and I was quite surprised to see it here on the island. My best guess is that it found its way into the Living Archives one day and ventured too close to the pond."

"We saw it just now," said Mai. "It led us here. But then it vanished."

"Yes, it does that," said Persephone. "Although why the Source saw fit to grant a cat the ability to teleport, I do not know. Very capricious of it."

Mai let out a surprised and rather loud laugh. But Tourmaline had stood silent all this time.

George wasn't sure he'd ever seen her so quiet and he'd definitely never seen her so forlorn. He wished more than anything that he could help her, but the only thing he could do was keep Persephone talking and hope that Tourmaline's memories would come back.

"I wonder," he said, "if living things are just more complex and so something more complex happens to them if they touch the Source."

Tourmaline looked at him then and shook her head minutely. She didn't want to tell her mother she couldn't remember her. She'd pretend. And if her memories never came back, then she'd pretend forever, although the thought of having to do that made her throat feel tight and her chest hurt.

It also gave her an idea. A desperate idea that, had she been able to remember what mothers are like, she would have known a mother would never agree to. She stared at Persephone's face hoping something, anything, even the tiniest scrap of familiarity would come to her. But it didn't.

Persephone was clearly considering George's idea. "That's a very astute observation, George. You may well be right! Cats do like to appear and disappear whenever it suits them, so maybe teleporting is a sort of magical version of catness."

Suddenly Tourmaline spoke. "Maybe we can trick the island."

Everyone looked at her.

"Maybe if one of us stays here, it would let the others leave." She looked at the woman who was her mother, even if she couldn't remember it. "We have a ship waiting."

She was not at all sure that they had a ship any more. Captain Violet might not even be on the island, and if she was, she might not be in any mood to have the children back on board, much less Persephone.

"I'll stay," she said. She wouldn't be able to hide the fact that she'd lost her memories forever. Not unless she stayed on the island and saved the others. Then she wouldn't have failed at rescuing her mother and she wouldn't have to look at her and feel the terrible emptiness where her memories should have been.

"It's out of the question," said Persephone.

"I'll stay here," Tourmaline said louder. "Do you hear

that, island? I'm staying right by the Source!" She took a step towards the edge of the precipice.

George had started breathing faster and faster. His hands had clenched into fists and suddenly he took a jerky step forwards. "It should be me. I'll stay."

Persephone stared at the children. "What is happening?"

George swallowed. "I'll stay," he said again. "You go with Tourmaline and Mai and I'll stay."

"George," said Tourmaline.

"I mean it!" he said, though his whole body was shaking. "I could study the Source like Persephone was doing. I've thought about working in the museum at the university lots of times."

"Both of you, stop," said Persephone. "This is all the most wonderfully brave thing I've ever heard in my life, but I absolutely can't let either of you do it." She looked at the two of them. "We're not even going to try."

Tourmaline closed her eyes briefly. There had to be a way.

Her eyes flew open. "The Source!" she said, getting even closer to the edge of the waterfall.

"Tourmaline, come away from there," said her mother, a note of panic in her voice.

"But the answer could be right there!" said Tourmaline, peering down. "Just like at the Living Archives when we had to look into the pond!"

Just then the cat appeared, blinking into existence between Tourmaline's feet and twining round her left leg.

Tourmaline wobbled on the brink of the waterfall.

Mai sucked in a breath.

George covered his mouth with both hands.

Persephone cried, "Tourmaline!" and dashed forwards to snatch her daughter back.

None of it had the slightest effect on Tourmaline overbalancing.

She slipped over the edge and plunged headfirst into the Source.

Chapter
Twenty-four

As Tourmaline fell, she thought about how she would never get her memories back now. She had only just got her real, actual mother back, and now she was going to lose her again. She was going to lose everything.

Then she hit the Source and couldn't think of anything except the bitter, shocking cold and the colours that slid in front of her eyes like ink and the thundering sound of the waterfall above and below and all around her. She kicked frantically, not knowing which way was up. The water (but it wasn't *quite* water, just like nothing on this island was quite what it seemed) roiled and frothed. Tiny bubbles pricked at her skin as her lungs began to burn, and then she was up, bursting through the surface, gasping for air, her head back, her arms and legs working to keep her afloat.

She swiped her hair from her eyes and looked around for a way out. But there was just the waterfall and the pool she was in right now. She couldn't touch the bottom. She couldn't see anything but the dark, earthy walls. Where the water went – if it even went, or came from, anywhere – she couldn't tell. Her teeth were chattering.

She looked up, and up, and up.

Far above her, three faces looked down. She had fallen so far, no one would be able to reach her. And she was cold.

"Tourmaline!" Her mother reached a hand down uselessly.

Tourmaline had no breath to call back.

"George!" said Persephone, taking his hands. "There's a length of rope over there in my camp."

She turned to Mai. "And … who are you?"

"I'm Tourmaline's other best friend – Mai."

"Lovely to meet you," said Persephone. "Run and get the blanket."

The children dashed away and Persephone dropped

to her knees at the edge of the waterfall. Tourmaline was panting and splashing below.

"Tourmaline, stop that at once! Lie on your back and float!"

Tourmaline didn't argue. She couldn't remember the woman yelling at her, but she knew love and concern when she heard it and she could see determination and passion in the woman's face.

So she did as she was told and soon found that, although she was cold, it was much easier to float than it was to dog paddle around in a circle or try to tread water.

"We'll have you out just as soon as we can," said Persephone, although her voice was just a bit too cheerful for Tourmaline's liking.

Persephone looked anxiously behind her and muttered something under her breath. Mai came running back first, carrying the blanket. George was close behind.

"What's the rope do?" asked Mai.

Persephone looked confused. "It's for Tourmaline to climb up."

George looked at her. "But isn't it magical?"

"Goodness, no," said Persephone as she lowered it down to Tourmaline. "It's just rope. Practical, though."

"What's the blanket for, then?" asked George.

"To dry her when she gets back up here."

George saw the good sense in this though it did feel a bit disappointing. He leaned (carefully) over the edge of the precipice just as the rope landed on Tourmaline's stomach.

"Climb up!" Persephone shouted down. "And we'll pull!"

Tourmaline couldn't feel her hands very well at this point, not to mention that her teeth were chattering so much that she honestly thought it might be blurring her vision. She fumbled with the rope.

"Hurry!" Persephone shouted.

Tourmaline seized the rope and started climbing while Persephone hauled her up with Mai and George helping. They were all out of breath when Tourmaline reached the top and slithered on to the floor like a seal, shaking hard but grinning widely.

Persephone scooped her up, hugged her tightly,

then held her out at arm's length. "Are you OK?"

Tourmaline nodded, her teeth still chattering, and as she looked into her mother's worried eyes, the thing that had started happening as she climbed up the rope finished happening. All her memories slid back into place as though they'd never left. Every birthday cake, every book Persephone had ever read to her, the time that Tourmaline had had an accident (yes, that kind) and Persephone had said never mind and that it happened to everyone, even the times when they'd argued because she'd been frustrated at her mother's secrets – they all slotted right back into Tourmaline's memory where they belonged. She blinked. And swallowed. Then shook herself a little bit to make sure all the pieces had got back into the right places.

Persephone pulled Tourmaline close again and she felt safe, right down inside her bones. Another alarming lump formed in her throat and her nose and eyes felt as though they might need to get very leaky very soon. She squeezed her mother tightly.

Persephone stroked her hair and Tourmaline remembered all the times her mother had done that over the years – when she had been cross or tired or frustrated or bored, or even when Persephone had done it absent-mindedly while reading a research paper held in her other hand.

Tourmaline caught George's eye and smiled the most relieved and exhausted and grateful smile even as she let out an audible sob, and George clenched both fists and pressed them together over his heart. Mai looked at the ceiling and blinked very fast several times.

Tourmaline and Persephone stood like that for several moments and Tourmaline basked, let herself float in it, and thought about nothing at all except the bliss of being a child who could trust her parent, until at last she lifted her head off her mother's shoulder and scrubbed her sleeve over her face.

George and Mai crowded around Tourmaline and rubbed her arms, and Persephone grabbed the blanket and wrapped her up in it.

George shrugged. "I suppose not everything can be solved by a magical artefact."

Persephone's brow wrinkled. "Goodness me, of course it can," she said. Immediately the blanket started to glow, a wonderful warm golden yellow, and steam started to rise from Tourmaline's clothes.

One by one, her curls shrank up to their usual coils. She breathed out. "I'm dry!"

Her clothes actually looked a little better for having had an impromptu wash, and it hadn't done her face any harm either. She smiled – a true, beaming, perfectly happy smile.

And then she remembered. They were still trapped.

The smile fell from her face just as footsteps came striding down the tunnel.

Persephone gathered the children behind her in alarm.

Everyone stared at the entrance to the tunnel on the other side of the cavern.

Mai hoped it was her mother, and then hoped it wasn't.

George put his hand on his chest and felt as though he really couldn't take any more shocks or even mild surprises that day.

Tourmaline called out, "Don't come in here!"

But it was too late.

Chapter
Twenty-five

Evelyn Coltsbody stepped into the cavern, an exultant look on his face. His gaze rested on Persephone and the children and he tilted his head.

He strolled up to them and smiled. "Tourmaline. Children. Persephone."

"Don't you Persephone me," said Tourmaline's mother.

George and Mai glanced at Tourmaline and then at each other. Tourmaline looked like a girl who had just seen both of her parents in the same place for the first time in her life after nearly drowning in the Source of all magic.

Evelyn Coltsbody ignored Persephone's tone and eyed the waterfall behind them. He looked like a man who had finally found exactly what he'd been looking for after years of searching.

"How fitting that the whole family is here for this," he said.

"We're not your family," said Tourmaline. "And you shouldn't have come here, because we're not going to let you have this island, or the Source, or even one tiny artefact."

Evelyn Coltsbody gave a surprised sort of laugh. "I doubt very much that you can stop me," he said. "But why on earth would you even want to? You're my daughter. If I own something, then one day, *you* will own it. Wouldn't you like that? Who wouldn't want to own this island?"

Tourmaline had been standing behind her mother, but now she stepped forwards (although Persephone kept hold of her hand and didn't let go).

"I wouldn't," said Tourmaline. "Nobody owns this island, it owns itself. I'm nothing like you, and I intend to stay that way."

Evelyn Coltsbody nodded. "I suppose it's all very well having ideals like that when you're young. It's easy to pretend that you're a good person when you've never had to make a choice that showed you otherwise." He smiled at her. "But you'll learn, as you get older."

"I don't want to learn that," said Tourmaline.

"That's quite enough," said Persephone to Evelyn Coltsbody, "and all perfectly pointless anyway. None of us can leave."

Evelyn Coltsbody let out a laugh which showed that he hadn't, as yet, grasped the severity of the situation, and Tourmaline stared at him. The mysterious Evelyn Coltsbody, also her (now less) mysterious father, possibly an enemy, creator of confusing feelings that she didn't have time to deal with.

"You should have listened to Tourmaline," continued her mother. "She was the only one of us with the wits to tell you to stay out of this cavern. Now you're here and you won't be able to get out. The only one who can leave is Fitzsimmons the cat. We're all trapped!"

An uncomfortable feeling, like electricity, suddenly filled the air in the silence that followed.

Evelyn Coltsbody's face changed quite dramatically

as first understanding, then fear, then desperation and panic took hold.

But Tourmaline stepped forwards, pulling out of her mother's grasp.

She had just had a brilliant idea. The most brilliant idea of all time. An idea that her mother had given her. It had to do with the cat. And it showed on her face.

Evelyn Coltsbody narrowed his eyes and stared at her, but her gaze was darting around the cavern. She was looking for Fitzsimmons.

Evelyn looked around the cavern too, after seeing Tourmaline's idea-face, and the very same idea apparently occurred to him. He turned and started to dash away.

"Mai!"

Tourmaline mimed something that looked like a thumb wiggling insistently. Everyone except Mai frowned. Mai, however, understood right away.

She yanked the watch out of her pocket, pointed it at Evelyn Coltsbody and pressed the button. He immediately froze mid-dash, except for his eyes, which blinked furiously. He tried to say something but Mai held the button down for another second, which shut him up nicely.

"I've had an idea!" Tourmaline announced.

Persephone stared at her daughter and then at Mai and the watch in her hand. "Where did you get that and what have you done? Well done, by the way."

"Just using one of his own tricks on him," said Tourmaline. She crossed her arms and looked at Evelyn Coltsbody. "Which, by the way, we wouldn't have been able to do if he hadn't been so careless with a magical artefact. These things are precious, in case you didn't know, and they're definitely not to be underestimated."

Something about the way Evelyn Coltsbody looked at her (deep annoyance, but also a thoughtful sort of look that might have included a smidgen of pride) made her wonder if perhaps he had meant to drop it. If he'd meant to leave it for her. If he'd been careless on purpose. Maybe he had.

Maybe not.

Persephone, meanwhile, was definitely looking at her daughter with pride.

"Well, what *is* your idea?" asked Mai.

Tourmaline took a deep breath. "I know how to get us out of here. And after that, how to stop anyone taking anything from this island."

Persephone's head tilted. "Except for the university, of course."

"No, Mother," said Tourmaline firmly. "Not even the university. That's really just the same as what everyone else on this island wants to do."

Persephone looked startled. "But we've only ever used the Source for *education*, Tourmaline. We wouldn't use magic to hurt anyone. In fact, we've never deliberately made any magical artefacts. There are strict regulations in place, which is why the Living Archives are completely secret in the first place."

"But we managed to find them," said Tourmaline.

"Well, yes," said Persephone.

"And aren't the books in the Archives magical artefacts?" asked Mai.

"Well, yes," said Persephone, more slowly, as though she were thinking about this for the first time, "but—"

"And aren't those magical artefacts why the dean gets so much money from students and those people at the fundraisers?" asked Tourmaline. "It's not really fair, when you think about it."

"I don't think—" said Persephone, even less certainly.

"I'm not sure the students should be paying for university at all," said George suddenly. He immediately swallowed and looked at the ground. But Tourmaline nodded.

"The island and everything on it needs to stay secret and hidden, like it always has been," she said resolutely. "It doesn't belong to anyone."

Persephone frowned uncertainly. It was an unusual expression for her but, Tourmaline thought, it really belonged on her face in this situation.

"Never mind that right now," said Mai. "How are we going to get out of this cavern?"

Chapter Twenty-six

"Are you sure about this?" asked Persephone, looking at Tourmaline.

Tourmaline stared down at Fitzsimmons the black-and-white cat in her arms, and the fresh scratch on the back of her hand.

"Yes," she said. "I mean, no. I mean, you said the cat can teleport, so—"

"Where do you think we'll appear?" asked George. His palm, resting on Tourmaline's shoulder, was sweating as he pictured an abrupt ejection from the cliff face of the island, followed by a long fall into the sea.

"Do you have enough of the spider silk?" Tourmaline asked her mother, who was touching Tourmaline's other shoulder.

What she had thought was fishing line, to which Persephone had earlier attached the apple, had turned out to be spider silk collected from the webs on the island. It was extremely strong and extremely flexible and, if Tourmaline's plan went to plan, it would be extremely important.

Persephone took her other hand off a still-frozen Evelyn Coltsbody and patted her pockets, which had several skeins of the silk in them. "I think so," she said. "And I'm certain everything will be just fine." She took hold of Evelyn's sleeve again and tried to tuck all the children under her arm at the same time.

Mai was standing in front of Tourmaline, both her hands on Tourmaline's forearms and one finger touching the cat's tail, in case that was important. "When do you think the cat will—"

But Mai never got to finish her question because Fitzsimmons, at that moment, decided that he had no further interest in being held tightly in Tourmaline's arms and teleported.

One second they were in the cavern, looking like a very strange family portrait, and the next they were blinking at the bright sunlight glinting off the sand.

Fitzsimmons leaped out of Tourmaline's arms as though he was about to sprint a hundred miles, then promptly sat down and began to wash his paw.

"It worked," said Tourmaline in stunned wonderment.

"We're on the beach?" said George, as though he couldn't quite believe it. "We're on the beach!" He did a sort of skip that showed he was very happy not to have to walk back through any of the things they had walked through on the way to the centre of the island and even happier to have survived teleportation in one piece.

Persephone let out a half-wild laugh and danced a jig.

Evelyn Coltsbody, still frozen, glowered at her.

"Now what?" Mai asked, shielding her eyes from the sun.

"Mai Cravenswood!"

Emiko Cravenswood came storming down the beach, tucking her clipboard under her arm. Her suit was a little salt-stained but the silver clip on her clipboard was still shiny. Mai bit her lip. George gave her a sympathetic look and felt fervently glad it wasn't his own mother in her place.

Emiko picked up her pace until she was practically running across the sand, made a beeline straight for Mai and collided with her in a fierce hug that knocked most of the breath out of them both.

"This is the most impossible, illogical place," Emiko said. "I have absolutely no idea how anyone could possibly understand it. The Agency is quite at its wits' end about what to do."

Tourmaline exchanged a quick, relieved glance with George.

"We," Emiko said sternly to her daughter, "are going to have a very long conversation about all of this, at a more appropriate time." She hugged Mai again, her eyes squeezed tight shut, then adjusted her suit, straightened her clipboard, and turned to the others.

"Is that," asked Emiko, indicating Evelyn Coltsbody, "who I think it is?"

"I expect so," said Tourmaline. "I expect you probably want to arrest him or something since you probably don't approve of his collection of magical artefacts or the fact that he wanted to use this island to make more."

Emiko frowned. "I expect I do."

"I have a plan, by the way," said Tourmaline. "One that will make it completely impossible for anybody else to find the island once we leave."

"So you don't have to destroy it," said Mai quickly.

Emiko looked at the two girls. "I'm listening."

Mai smiled, Tourmaline explained and George hoped that it wouldn't take too long because he was very hungry and had really had enough.

"In that case," said Emiko, when Tourmaline had finished, "I agree that the Agency for the Investigation and Classification of Magical Artefacts will forego destroying the island, which was proving rather difficult anyway. *As long as* everyone else here agrees that as far as the rest of the world is concerned, neither the island itself nor the Agency actually exist."

She eyed everyone meaningfully.

Persephone made a small, pained sound.

George patted her hand.

Emiko raised her eyebrows.

"We all agree," said Tourmaline quickly. "Don't we?" She widened her eyes at her mother.

Persephone took a sad, measured breath. "I give you my word," she said.

"Is it me," said George, who had been adjusting his feet on the sand for a few moments, "or is the island starting to tilt?"

Just then Captain Violet burst out of the jungle undergrowth closely followed by Quintalle, Miracle and Dexta.

"The island's moving!" the captain bellowed. "Abandon island!"

Tourmaline hurriedly gestured to Persephone, who pulled the skeins of spider silk out of her pocket and began to hand them out. "I have a plan!" Tourmaline shouted to the crew. "We have to use this to tether the island to the ship! We're going to move it!"

"Sorry," said Dexta as she ran past Tourmaline and splashed into the water. "We have to save our own hides."

Tourmaline threw her hands up as the whole crew waded into the sea. "Stop! Captain Violet, don't you want to be one of the only people in the world who knows where this island is?"

The crew slowed down. Captain Violet stopped and turned. "I do like that idea," she said.

"I thought you might," said Tourmaline. She lost her footing and sat down hard. "I also think the island's trying to tip us off. We have to hurry."

The crew waded back on to the beach and Persephone quickly handed silk thread to each of them. "Tie it to something on the island," she said. "We'll tie the other end to *The Hunter*. We're going to tow this island to the middle of nowhere and no one will have a map to find it."

As if it knew she was talking about it, the island gave a sudden lurch, the beach where they all stood tilting further downwards. A hot-air balloon of sky-blue silk that had been cut to shreds came tumbling out of the jungle and rolled along the beach. Mai dodged it, then watched it continue across the sand (which wasn't moving at all, but staying completely flat on the island as it tilted). This made George's brain ache, so he looked at Evelyn Coltsbody, who was watching the basket as several interesting, possibly magical items spilled out of it and were lost on the sand.

"Yours?" asked George.

Evelyn Coltsbody blinked at him balefully.

A broken hang glider followed the balloon, one wing flapping loosely as it bounced off the edge of the island.

"That was mine," Persephone said sadly.

Tourmaline ran and tied her thread to a sturdy tree. The island was tilting so far now that she had to lean forwards, digging her feet into the soft earth.

"Tourmaline!" Mai was sliding down the beach, a look of terror on her face.

"Hold on to your thread!" Tourmaline shouted at her, as Quintalle and Emiko started to slide too. She dug her feet in to wedge herself but she was falling, the island tipping all the way down now. It had had enough and wanted them gone.

"Everyone, hold on to your threads!" Her stomach tried to retreat to safe, horizontal land but it was no good, she was picking up speed.

Captain Violet tumbled past and then Tourmaline was in the sea that surrounded the island, then out of it, skimming over the surface as the ground tipped until it was vertical. Persephone shot past with a look of grim determination on her face and Tourmaline wrapped her thread round her wrist once more for luck as she shot off the edge, falling into space, the ordinary blue sea rushing up at her as the sky and the island retreated.

Dexta whooped somewhere below her and then Tourmaline was sailing down towards the ocean and the ships anchored there, her stomach flipping, her heart swooping, her thread unspooling from her wrist.

A thin, high-pitched scream zoomed past. It belonged to George, whose arms and legs were pinwheeling out of sync as he fell. The rope they'd used to climb up was nowhere to be seen, not that anybody would have had time to use it.

Tourmaline saw Emiko somehow land neatly on the deck of *The Hunter* along with Evelyn Coltsbody, and then the water was right underneath her, sparkling white and blue and knocking her breath right out of her with its cold. It bobbed her back and forth as she surfaced, shaking her hair out of her eyes.

Several feelings and thoughts bobbed around inside her, including relief, eagerness to get on with the rest of her plan, a fervent wish to be dry for more than two hours at a time, the fact that she was hungrier than she'd ever been in her life or ever wanted to be again, and surprise that she had made it this far and no one had even got *that* close to dying.

Chapter Twenty-seven

Tourmaline floated on her back, watching the island slowly tilt itself back to a more normal angle, before she made it on to *The Hunter*'s lifeboat and then on to *The Hunter* itself with everyone else, dripping water on to the deck as they all looked at her.

"What happened to the rope?" asked Mai, looking at the artefact they'd used to climb up to the island, which was now haphazardly coiled on the deck. Nobody answered her. Nobody really knew.

"Tie the thread to the ship," said Tourmaline. "We're going to tow the island away to somewhere no one will find it. Too many people know that it's here now."

George ran his fingers down the fine silken thread he

was holding, the other end of which he'd tied to a large stone on the beach. They each fastened their threads to the mast, and Captain Violet put her fists on her hips and looked down at Tourmaline.

"Where to?"

Tourmaline smiled. "You'd better fetch your maps and ask Mai. She's the expert."

The captain nodded at Miracle, who ran off to fetch the maps, ruffling Mai's hair on the way. Mai watched Miracle run thoughtfully, then a slow smile spread across her face.

Once Mai had selected a remote location and a course was plotted, Emiko announced that she would be staying on *The Hunter* to supervise 1) the delivery of Evelyn Coltsbody and the pocket watch to the AICMA ship since nobody wanted him aboard *The Hunter*, 2) the delivery of the offending island to its hiding place where it could safely exist without people having to worry about household items developing startling powers, and 3) Mai having a bath and a hot meal and a good night's sleep in that order and no questions about it.

Persephone agreed wholeheartedly with 3 being

applied to Tourmaline and George, although she couldn't help but mutter something about the university and her life's work when it came to 2.

Captain Violet took the wheel and Tourmaline stood next to her, the wind blowing in her face as the ship pointed its bow towards open waters.

"You do understand why we're doing this?" asked Tourmaline.

"Not entirely," said the captain. "But I daresay you're about to explain whether I like it or not. Your mother doesn't seem very pleased that she can't steal the Source for her university."

"She's not," said Tourmaline, ignoring the word "steal". "I think she's probably got a lot to think about when it comes to the Source. Were you ever going to just let Evelyn Coltsbody have the island? Didn't you want it for yourself?" She was thinking about his very destroyed hot-air balloon. Its demise would have certainly resulted in him being at Captain Violet's mercy when it came to leaving the island.

"What do you think?" asked the captain.

"Were you going to use the Source to make a lot

of magical artefacts?"

"Probably," said Captain Violet cheerfully.

"Definitely," said Dexta, who was climbing the rigging above their heads.

The captain side-eyed Tourmaline. "Excellent work getting over that chasm, by the way. You'll have to explain to me how you did that some time."

Tourmaline side-eyed the captain. "I think that should stay between George and Mai and myself. No offence."

"None taken," said Captain Violet.

*

When the children emerged from their baths, wet-haired and with a fuzzy warm feeling in their limbs, the long-awaited food was ready. Quintalle had brought roasted vegetables and mountains of mashed potatoes, bread and, somehow, a gigantic chocolate cake out on to the deck and Miracle had laid out thick rugs.

Dexta dumped a collection of possibly stolen silverware on the middle of the rug and they all tucked in. Persephone and Emiko sat at one end engaged in a conversation about parenting that neither Tourmaline nor Mai particularly wanted to hear. It then turned into a conversation about magic and artefacts which no one had any choice but to hear because it got very lively and seemed to give both women more to think about than they possibly cared to.

The three children sat at the other end of the rugs and ate until they felt full and dazed and sleepy. George turned his spoon upside down and licked the last bit of chocolate cake off it so he could see his own reflection.

"You both look different," said George. "I don't."

"I don't look different, do I?" asked Tourmaline.

"I think you do," said George. "There's something shiny about you. Both of you."

"That's just the bath," said Tourmaline.

George shrugged. "Maybe. But I don't look shiny. I don't look any different at all. I thought I might after everything."

"OK, you don't look any different," said Mai. "But do you *feel* different?"

George thought about it. "I think I do."

Mai shrugged. "That's what matters, don't you think?"

George blinked, helped himself to a sliver more chocolate cake, and thought about it until he decided that Mai was right.

"How long will it take to get to where we're leaving the island?" asked Tourmaline.

"Ten days, or maybe a week if the winds are good," said Mai.

Tourmaline glanced at her mother to check she wasn't looking, then slathered mashed potato on some bread. "You're very good at this, you know. You could have your own ship one day."

Mai smiled the sort of delighted smile that people smile when you've given them the exact right sort of compliment.

Persephone stood up. "That was magnificent," she said. "Thank you, Quintalle. Now I think the children need to sleep."

"We've really been managing quite well without anyone telling us when to go to sleep," said Tourmaline in a dignified way, which was only a little spoiled by the smear of chocolate cake on her face.

"Perhaps a rest for a short while might be a good

idea," said George, who was feeling full and sleepy and didn't mind a grown-up telling him what to do.

"Fine," said Tourmaline, as though she was only doing it for him, and not because she could barely keep her eyes open.

They left the adults on deck and went to their old room, where someone had put up three hammocks. Tourmaline climbed into one (it only took three attempts) and settled herself down. The hammock swung gently. "George?"

"Mm." He already sounded half asleep.

"I never did thank you for what you did – when you offered to stay on the island instead of me."

"It was nothing," said George, in a tone of voice that said he knew very well that it was quite the opposite of nothing.

"It really wasn't," said Tourmaline. "I think you were very brave."

"Tourmaline," he said. "You told Captain Violet that she'd be one of the few people in the world who knew where the island was."

"Did I?" said Tourmaline carelessly.

"You did. But you know, I couldn't help but see Persephone giving you a tiny blue flower when she put all that spider silk in her pockets."

"Hmm," said Tourmaline. "You're right. She did."

"And was that flower a forget-me-not? It certainly looked like one."

"It was." She didn't even try to sound innocent. In fact, she grinned, and George could hear it.

"Tell me," said George.

"It will make Captain Violet and the crew completely forget where they put the island. Evelyn Coltsbody too. He's going to hate that."

"I see," said George. "Well played, Tourmaline."

Chapter Twenty-eight

The next thing Tourmaline knew she was waking up with the sun coming in at a completely different angle through the porthole. She had the sense that she had been deeply asleep for a very long time.

She blinked and quietly climbed down (George was still asleep but Mai's hammock was empty) and went up to the deck. The sun was high in the sky and *The Hunter* was clipping along with full sails.

Emiko Cravenswood was standing on deck with Quintalle and Miracle, wearing crew clothes instead of her suit. All three of them had their heads bent over Emiko's clipboard and she was pointing with a pen and saying something about organizing the ship's rations and increasing productivity levels.

Persephone and Captain Violet were at the wheel, and Tourmaline could hear Persephone telling the captain a tale about her trip to the Valley of the Queens and the clues she had found there that had led her to the island. Captain Violet was interrupting her to add in her own stories about artefacts she had hunted and how she had once been chased through the lobby of a very exclusive hotel by a rival hunter who suspected her of having stolen a magical ferret – which had turned out to be very non-magical, and had bitten Captain Violet multiple times.

The captain was just showing Persephone the scars when they saw Tourmaline.

"There you are!" said Persephone. She climbed down the ladder to her daughter, and Tourmaline noticed that Mai was up in the crow's nest with Dexta, blue hair and black blowing together in the wind. Beyond them, the island moved gently, like an enormous balloon being towed by a child. The skeins of silk made faint, silvery lines in the air between *The Hunter* and the island.

Persephone joined her at the stern of the ship and they both leaned on the railing, looking out and pondered the strangeness going on overhead.

"I think," said Persephone, "that it's the lack of a shadow that's most disconcerting."

"For me," said Tourmaline, "it might have been the talking trees, meeting my father, or the magical portal mirrors."

"You've had a very eventful few days," said Persephone. "How are you feeling?"

"Like I've been put into a sack and shaken very thoroughly for some time."

"I meant about meeting your father," said Persephone.

"Oh, him," said Tourmaline. She looked up at a seagull that was hovering over the ship.

"I'm sorry I didn't tell you," said Persephone quietly.

"I wish you had," said Tourmaline. "But I can sort of see why you didn't. I thought I needed to know who he was or else I wouldn't really know who *I* am. But I don't think that any more. I know who I am. Or who I want to try to be."

"That's a fine thing to know," said Persephone, sounding impressed.

"I still have some questions about him, though," said Tourmaline.

The wind ruffled Persephone's curls and she nodded. "Of course."

"Also, will the university be OK without more Source water?"

Persephone paused, very briefly. "It will have to be."

"You could have told me about it all – the Living Archives and the Source and your mission," said Tourmaline. "I'm not a little girl any more."

Persephone looked at her for a long moment. "I can see that now," she said. "You know, when you're someone's mother, you have to keep adjusting the idea of whose mother you are in your mind as they change and grow up. Sometimes you forget to do it, or you don't want to do it, or you … you don't take the time to notice that you should do it." She smiled, a little sadly.

"It sounds quite difficult," said Tourmaline.

"It is," said Persephone. "It's much harder than being an archaeologist or a tenured professor."

"I'm not sure I'd really like to be a mother," said Tourmaline.

Persephone smiled. "Then don't be one. You can be anything you like. I have mentioned that before, haven't I?"

Tourmaline nodded. "Yes, you've mentioned it."

"Good. And now I'm going to promise that I'll always tell you exactly where I'm going and why I'm going there from now on."

Tourmaline thought about promising the same thing, then concluded it would be a terrible idea.

"Also," said Persephone, "there's a mission at home that seems like quite an adventure and I think I should like to try that out while I still can."

"Really?" said Tourmaline, looking across at her mother.

"The mission is you," said Persephone and her eyes might have been shining.

Tourmaline blinked. Her heart was very full and it might have overflowed if she'd done anything else. She reached for her mother's hand and Persephone squeezed it tight. She smiled at Tourmaline and Tourmaline sniffed hard and smiled back, very much liking the look in her mother's eyes, which was love and pride and a little bit of wonderment.

Tourmaline searched those dark brown eyes, an alarming thought suddenly occurring to her. "You won't give up exploring, though, will you?"

Persephone looked equally alarmed. "Goodness, no! Of course not."

Tourmaline grinned and breathed a sigh of relief. Persephone with her and really present some of the time would be wonderful, but Persephone there *all* of the time might not leave room for either of them to have other adventures, and Tourmaline found that she really did want her own adventures.

Persephone looked back out to sea. "There's a motorcycle in the hold that looks very familiar."

Tourmaline also hastily looked back out to sea. "Professor Aladeus is working with Evelyn Coltsbody, you know," she said.

"Is he indeed?" said her mother, sounding a lot less impressed than she had with anything else so far.

"He told the dean a rescue party had been sent for you, but he was lying. He might have got Professor Sharma mixed up in it too."

Persephone's grip on the railing tightened. "Well, we'll see about that when we get home."

Tourmaline was surprised to find that when her mother said the word *home*, her heart gave a little pull in her chest. It might be quite nice to go home, to see Josie, even to see the museum. Artefacts were not always what she had thought, and neither were quite a few other things. What else out there in the world might surprise her?

From across the deck, George watched Persephone and Tourmaline talking with their heads close together. He tilted his own head, wondering if he would ever talk to his own mother that way. Possibly not, he concluded, but maybe it didn't have to be a mother. Maybe it could be a Josie or a someone he hadn't even met yet. Or maybe even a stepfather.

Chapter
Twenty-nine

That night, Tourmaline was lying in her hammock, her hands behind her head, while the stars twinkled prettily outside the porthole. George and Mai stood on the other side of the door, having a discussion about magic. It had become quite heated, and seemed to be keeping them in the corridor.

"I'm just saying," said George, "that there's a scientific reason for all this."

"No, there isn't," said Mai flatly.

"I'll prove it!" said George.

"Go on, then," said Mai.

"One day, I will," said George. "I'm going to study this when I grow up and then you'll see…"

George carried on talking very earnestly and

Tourmaline thought she heard a sigh from Mai, but her attention was whipped away from her friends by something inside the room.

A strange light had filled her hammock. Thinking that more stars had appeared, or the moon was full tonight, she looked out of the porthole (even though she'd known, deep down, that this wasn't moonlight).

The illumination was coming from behind her head. She brought her hands down and stared at them. They were glowing. Faint colours swirled within the light, which seemed to come from underneath her skin. The colours looked very much like oil on water, like a swirling rainbow, like … a certain waterfall that was not quite a waterfall that she'd fallen into recently.

She turned her hands over and wondered if anyone else had ever plunged into the Source and spent quite some time floating around in it and, if so, what had happened to them?

She took a deep breath and raised her voice. "George? Mai? Could you come in here for a minute, please?"

Look out for
Tourmaline's next
adventure, coming
Spring 2024!

Acknowledgements

Many thanks go to the following people: my friend and critique partner, Michelle Krys. I've never written a book she hasn't read, sometimes more than once, and this has been going on for twelve years now. Needless to say, she's put up with a lot.

My agent, Anne Clark. Without her, Tourmaline wouldn't have found a home with a wonderful publisher. I'll be forever grateful that I get to carry on doing this for a job because of her.

My editor, Mattie Whitehead (thank you, thank you, thank you!), along with Lauren Ace at Little Tiger, for loving Tourmaline and wanting to bring her story to reality (and working so hard to make that happen).

The whole team at Little Tiger – Pip Johnson, Summer Lanchester, Dannie Price, Demet Hoffmeyer, George Hanratty, Charlie Moyler and Kimberley Chen. Thanks to Nicola O'Connell, Tourmaline will be sailing overseas from the UK too! As many gingery biscuits as you can eat for all of you.

Thanks to Anna Bowles for thorough and thoughtful copy editing, to Leena Lane for perfecting the final details on the proofread, to Kat Cassidy for the fantastic cover reveal graphic, and to Sharon King-Chai for the truly magnificent cover and map.

About the Author

Ruth Lauren lives in the West Midlands in England with her family. When she isn't writing, she's almost certainly reading, playing D&D (badly) or falling down the rabbit hole of whatever she's currently obsessed with. Ruth's acclaimed middle grade novel *Prisoner of Ice and Snow* was chosen by the American Booksellers' Association as a top debut of the season, and its sequel *Seeker of the Crown* earned a starred Kirkus review.

🐦 @ruthlaurenbooks | 📷 @ruthlaurenbooks